ACCUSED (AMISH ROMANCE MYSTERY)

AMISH SECRET WIDOWS' SOCIETY BOOK 3

SAMANTHA PRICE

CHAPTER 1

My fruit is better than gold, yea, than fine gold; and my
revenue than choice silver. I lead in the way of righteousness, in
the midst of the paths of judgment:
That I may cause those that love me to inherit substance;
and I will fill their treasures.
Proverbs 8:19-21

Feeling foolish was the last thing that Angela expected to feel when she came to Lancaster County. She was assured by her *Ant* Elsa-May that Robert would be a match for her. That was the sole reason she agreed to correspond with the man. Now, after at least forty letters and many months had passed, she sat in his living room while he sat glaring across from her as if she'd escaped from some far away insane asylum.

"How is it that you know nothing of me?" Angela

pulled a bundle of letters, which were tied with a purple ribbon, from her drawstring bag. "You've written me all these." Somewhere in Angela's embarrassed fog she hoped that if he saw the letters it might bring something to mind.

He glanced at the letters in Angela's outstretched hand and gave a dismissive wave. "I know nothing of them." His dark brown eyes looked directly into hers. "Is it possible that you have the wrong person?" His voice hinted of desperation.

Angela shook her head and placed the letters in her lap. "I just can't understand it." She drew one of the letters from the pile and pointed to the name and address on the back of it. "That's your name and this is your address. I've been writing to you at this address for months."

Robert bounded to his feet and ran his long fingers through his thick, dark hair. "Give me a look at one of those letters." He examined the letter for a moment, shook his head and said, "That has to be the only explanation."

"What?" Angela asked again, "What has to be the only explanation?

Robert either didn't hear her or chose to ignore her. He strode purposely toward his front door and yelled, "Jacob, come here."

"I'm busy, *Onkel* Robert. Can I talk to you later?"

Angela hurried to the door and stood behind Robert. She stood on her tiptoes to look over his shoulder at Jacob, who was in the field closest to the *haus.* Angela had heard of Jacob, the nephew that Robert had taken in and cared for as his own. Robert always mentioned in his letters how much he liked Jacob.

"Now," Robert repeated, firmly, pressing his hands into his hips.

Jacob lifted up the long rein attached to the horse. "I'm busy with the horses."

It appeared to Angela, from all the straps attached to the horse, that Jacob was breaking the horse into harness.

"I said now, Jacob." Robert moved out of the doorway and onto the porch.

Angela stayed a little behind Robert and watched Jacob walk toward the *haus* shuffling his feet.

"Jacob, this is Miss Bontreger."

"Hello, Miss Bontreger." Jacob smiled when he looked at Angela.

"Hello, Jacob." Angela noticed that when Jacob's eyes moved back to Robert, the smile left his face altogether.

"Do you know anything about letters? Have you been writing letters to Miss Bontreger pretending to be me?"

Angela's mouth fell open. *So that's what happened.* She was glad she did not gasp audibly; she felt foolish enough just being there.

Jacob glanced over his *onkel's* shoulder toward Angela then looked to the ground. "Well, I thought it would make you happy if you had a *fraa*. Maybe then you won't be angry all the time."

Angela moved to stand next to Robert and out of the corner of her eye she saw that Robert was red in the face with anger.

In a controlled tone Robert said, "I am only angry because you do things such as these. If you didn't continue to do these things then I would have no cause for unhappiness or anger. Go to your room."

Jacob dragged his feet past Robert and Angela.

"Wait a moment," Robert said.

Jacob stopped still and looked up at his *onkel* with large, sad eyes.

"Don't you think you have someone else you should apologize to?" Robert asked.

Jacob looked up at Angela. "Sorry, Miss Bontreger."

Angela did the best she could to force a smile. She couldn't help but feel sorry for Jacob, being reprimanded in front of a visitor. "Apology accepted, Jacob."

Jacob walked into the house.

Robert turned to Angela, red-faced. "No words, I simply have no words." He put a hand to his forehead. "No words except to say that I'm very sorry. I hope you can forgive my rudeness earlier. I had no idea who you were and we're not used to having visitors."

"That's quite alright. My visit must have come as a shock."

"Jacob and I keep to ourselves most of the time." Robert ran his eyes up and down Angela. "Come back inside and I'll fix some tea and cookies."

Angela put her hand to her heart. "I feel terrible for intruding on you like this. I feel silly."

Robert put his hand up. "Not another word. It's me who's in the wrong – completely. Please, come back inside."

While they drank tea Robert asked, "So, how many letters did he send you?"

"Quite a few and over some months. He even sent me money to travel here to meet him, I mean you did – *ach*, it's a bit confusing. I'll give you the money back, of course."

Robert shook his head. "So that's where his money went. Nonsense, you'll not give anything back. I feel deeply troubled with the disruption that Jacob and I have caused you."

Angela forced another smile even though she felt sick to the stomach. "No harm done."

Robert disappeared into the kitchen then came back with a tray of cookies.

Angela brought the teacup to her lips, saddened that the letters weren't from Robert. He was exactly the kind of *mann* she would have liked. He was tall, strong and responsible. *Robert must be a caring mann to have looked after Jacob all this time. Elsa-May was right about him. I wonder what he thinks of me? Seems he's not looking for a fraa at all,* Angela thought.

Robert put both hands over his face and rubbed his forehead. "I don't know what I'm going to do with that boy."

"His heart was in the right place. He was trying to make you happy."

"I wouldn't have dared to do a thing like that when I was a *youngin.* I would've got such a hiding I wouldn't have been able to sit for a week."

Angela knew she was partly responsible. She should have realized that it was a child writing to her, but the writing style was so mature. "Are you going to punish him?"

"I'll stop him looking after the horses for a week. He

likes to train the horses. We've got a new one out there at the moment. The gray one he was working with."

"Did you teach him to break horses in?"

"I showed him the basic things, but he has a knack of knowing how to handle the horses and they respond well to him."

"*Jah*, keeping him away from the horses will upset him and make him think twice about doing such a thing again." Angela was glad that the boy escaped a whipping. She would feel horrid if such a thing happened on her account.

CHAPTER 2

Fear thou not; for I am with thee: be not dismayed; for I am thy God: I will strengthen thee; yea, I will help thee; yea, I will uphold thee with the right hand of my righteousness.
Isaiah 41:10

The Day Before

IT WAS A MOST beautiful day in Lancaster County. The sun was high in the sky and a gentle breeze kissed Emma's face. As her buggy clip-clopped forward, Emma became transfixed by the shadows made on the road as the sunlight filtered through the trees. She was glad the cold weather was over; spring was well and truly here.

Emma knew as soon as she arrived at Elsa-May and Ettie's *haus* that Ettie was in a particularly disagreeable mood. The elderly sisters had lived together for years from the time shortly after both their husbands died. Elsa-May was the elder and usually the more outspoken of the two. Ettie mostly agreed with everything that Elsa-May said. From their appearance, no one would guess that the two sisters were related. Elsa-May was a large, robust woman whereas Ettie was small and thin. Emma guessed them to be in their late seventies or early eighties – she never asked and they never told.

When Emma tied up her horse and entered the sisters' house, she noticed that there was barely a smile on Ettie's face. Emma was at the house for the widows' meeting. The group of five widows met together at least once a week and enjoyed a time where they were free to speak whatever was on their minds. Cake and sweets of all kinds were a vital ingredient at the meetings.

"What's the matter, Ettie? You don't look very happy," Emma said.

"Listen to what Elsa-May has to say and see what you think of it," Ettie said.

"I've been writing to a niece of mine, Angela Bontreger; she's twenty eight and has never married. I told her about Robert Geiger. I simply encouraged her to write to him." Elsa-May looked pleased with herself and bit off a portion of chocolate brownie.

Ettie narrowed her eyes at her *schweschder*. "You could have told me that before today, Elsa-May. Do you think that's a *gut* idea, to have Angela throw herself at him? Just because two people are Amish and aren't married doesn't mean they are going to get along with one another."

"Where does your niece live, Elsa-May?" Silvie asked as she pushed a few blonde strands of hair back from her pretty face tucking them under her prayer *kapp*.

"She lives in Bloomfield."

"Is she your niece too, Ettie?" Maureen asked since Elsa-May and Ettie were sisters. Maureen had always been a close friend to Emma and it was she who invited Emma to join the widows' group shortly after Emma's husband died.

Ettie shook her head and kept looking down at her needlework. "*Nee*, she's Elsa-May's late husband's niece, his *schweschder's dochder*."

"How long has she been writing to him, Elsa-May?" Silvie asked as she blinked her attractive, blue eyes. Just like Maureen, Silvie had been widowed for quite some time. Both Maureen and Silvie were in their early thirties, slightly older than Emma.

Elsa-May chuckled. "She's been writing to him for around five months and he's invited her to visit. She's very excited. She arrives tomorrow."

Ettie pressed her lips tightly together and shook her head.

"What's the matter now, Ettie?" Elsa-May asked.

Ettie lowered her needlework and looked at Elsa-May. "No *gut* will come of it."

Elsa-May snorted. "Come of what?"

"Meddling. Nothing *gut* ever comes of meddling."

"Nonsense. We meddle all the time." Elsa-May laughed. "That's what we do."

The two sisters often ended up annoyed with each other; it was mostly Ettie who backed down before things became too heated.

Emma spoke up to try and soothe things between the two *schweschders*. "What harm can it do, Ettie? If they meet and don't get along, then that's one man who she can cross off her list. Who knows? They might get along just fine and get married."

Emma's words weren't of much use as Ettie still had a stony expression on her face and her lips were so tightly pressed together that they formed a thin line.

It seemed as though Elsa-May could not keep the smile from her face despite Ettie's disapproval. "You'll all get to meet my niece of course. She's a lovely girl."

Silvie brought her teacup to her lips and before she took a sip, she asked, "Why has she never married?"

"She's quite shy, which doesn't help matters. Her *mudder* told me she was in love with a boy and was holding out for him for the longest time, but he married someone else."

"That's sad," Maureen said.

"There might not be too many *menner* in Bloomfield," Silvie said.

"If *Gott* wants her to be married, He'll put someone in her path," Ettie said. "It's not for us to do His work."

"You'd do something to help yourself though, wouldn't you, Ettie? So just keep out of things that don't concern you." Elsa-May folded her arms across her chest.

Emma was shocked by Elsa-May's words and glanced at the other widows' faces to see that they were also startled by her words.

Ettie shot her head up and dropped her needlework into her lap. The tension between the sisters hung heavily in the room.

Emma quickly spoke again to avoid any further unpleasantness. "Maybe that's what *Gott* has done now, Ettie. He's put it in Elsa-May's head to encourage Angela to write to Robert. Angela didn't have to write to him. No one forced her to do it. Now, Robert's invited Angela to meet him."

"It's still okay for Angela to stay with you, isn't it, Emma?" Elsa-May asked.

"*Jah,* I'll be pleased with the company. I get lonely in the big old *haus* with just me and Growler." Growler was Emma's cat that she had reluctantly taken in when his previous owner was murdered just months ago.

Emma turned to see Ettie staring at her open-mouthed. "What is it, Ettie?"

"You knew about all this?" Ettie asked.

"Yesterday Elsa-May asked if Angela could stay for a time. I said she could stay as long as she wanted."

Elsa-May quickly added, "She can't stay here, can she? Our *haus* is barely big enough for the both of us at times."

Maureen cleared her throat in a nervous manner. "Speaking of *haus* guests, do you still have your *schweschder* staying with you, Silvie?"

"*Jah,* she's still there. I suppose it's nice to have a little company, but I'd most likely prefer to borrow Growler as a *haus* guest." Silvie gave a little laugh. "Sabrina's like a bee in a bottle; she always wants to go places and do things. I let her take the buggy by herself. She's out most days. I have no idea where she goes; I'm just glad for the peace. I know she's scouting around looking for a husband; that's for sure and for certain. Before she goes home, she's making sure that she's met all the boys in the community."

The widows laughed.

"Have you heard from that nephew of mine, Silvie?" Elsa-May asked.

"*Jah*, Bailey writes me twice a week. Still hasn't said anything about visiting me or joining the Amish. Does he still write to you two?" Silvie asked of Elsa-May and Ettie.

"We get the occasional letter. He speaks fondly of you, Silvie," Elsa-May said.

Silvie's cheeks turned a shade of pink and she looked down into the chocolate cake in her lap.

"You can't push him, you know," Ettie said.

"I know, Ettie. It was he who suggested that he might join us in the future. I would never push him into something. It would never work that way. He has to want to join us." Silvie swallowed hard. "He has asked me to visit him."

"You should go," Elsa-May said.

Silvie met Elsa-May and Ettie's *Englischer* nephew, Bailey Rivers, months ago when he was working on a case in Lancaster County. Bailey Rivers is an undercover detective and at the time Bailey and Silvie met, Bailey was working undercover and staying within the community under the pretense of wishing to join the community.

Bailey assured Silvie that his deception was necessary for his job. Silvie suggested that he change his job. Bailey had hinted that he might become Amish when he finished the case that he was working on. The only catch was that the investigation had already taken him many years and there was no telling how much longer it would take.

"Are you unsure of leaving Sabrina alone in the *haus* when you visit him?" Emma asked. Sabrina was Silvie's *schweschder* who had been visiting her on an extended stay, mainly because there were more *menner* to choose from in Lancaster County than in her hometown.

"*Jah*, partly that and partly that I haven't traveled much outside the community." Silvie gave a little laugh. "I'm a little nervous travelling alone, finding my way and that kind of thing."

"Do you want me to go with you?" Maureen asked.

"*Denke*, Maureen, but if I go I should probably go alone. I might take you up on it. I'll have a think about it."

"The offer's there if you want it. Just give me some notice so I can arrange time off from work." Maureen was a likeable woman with a large smile. She was a generous woman in heart, body and mind. Everyone who knew her liked her.

CHAPTER 3

Through faith we understand that the worlds were framed by the word of God, so that things which are seen were not made of things which do appear.
Hebrews 11:3

EMMA HAD PREPARED one of her upstairs bedrooms for Angela's stay. She had freshly washed the sheets, washed the floor, dusted the furniture and opened the window to air the room out. It had been a long time since Emma had visitors.

"Emma."

Emma heard Wil calling her name from the bottom of the stairs.

"Hello, Wil. I'm expecting Angela here shortly. I'm just upstairs fixing her room. I'll be down there in one minute."

Emma hurried down the stairs, anxious to see Wil. Even though they saw each other every day, her heart still skipped a beat whenever she saw him.

"It'll do you *gut* to have someone staying with you. I'll make myself scarce. I've just brought that broken kitchen chair back to you."

"*Denke*, Wil. It looks as *gut* as new."

"It is. I've put new rods in the sides. It's stronger than when it was new. Do you want it back in the kitchen?" Before Emma could open her mouth, Wil was walking into the kitchen carrying the chair.

"*Jah*, in the kitchen." Emma placed her hands on her hips as she watched Wil's strong body walk away from her. She knew things hadn't been easy for Wil. He wanted to marry her way before now, but Emma was worried that an acceptable time hadn't yet passed after Levi had died, to marry. She was thankful that Wil had been patient.

"I'll go before Angela comes, so you two can get to know each other by yourselves without me around."

"*Nee*, you don't have to do that. Stay and have the midday meal with us."

"I've got errands to run this afternoon and I'd best start them now." Wil walked toward Emma and gave her a quick kiss on the forehead before he strode out the door.

Emma stood on the porch and watched Wil's buggy drive up the road. Just as his buggy was a speck in the distance, a taxi appeared beside it traveling toward Emma's *haus*. *I wonder if this is Angela*, Emma thought. The taxi continued right to her front door. Emma stepped down from the porch to meet Angela.

Angela opened the taxi door. She had a dark green

dress in a full style, which was more gathered than most of the Amish women wore in Lancaster County. Emma noticed that the prayer *kapp* was a little smaller and made of sheer material. The white apron she wore was the same as the aprons that Emma was used to. Angela was a tall girl with dark hair and dark eyes. She was not unattractive.

Emma reached out her hands. "Angela?"

"*Jah*, and you're Emma?"

The two ladies gave each other a small kiss on the side of the cheek. The taxi driver dropped a bag at Angela's feet. "Would you like me to take it inside for you?" he asked Angela.

"*Nee.* I can do it, *denke.*"

"Here let me take it." Emma picked up the bag and Angela followed her into the *haus* as the taxi drove away.

"I've got you in one of the upstairs bedrooms. Follow me," Emma said.

As Angela followed her up the stairs and said, "I can't thank you enough for this, Emma."

Emma glanced back at her. "It'll be *gut* to have some company." Emma passed her own room and saw that Growler was asleep in the middle of the bed. She stopped in the doorway and nodded her head in his direction. "That's my cat, Growler. He'll most likely ignore you. He ignores me most of the time unless I'm late with his dinner."

"By the look of him I would say that you're never late with his dinner. He must be the largest cat I've ever seen. My cats are nowhere near that size."

Emma continued to the next doorway. "This is your

room." She placed the suitcase on the bed. "You can unpack now if you like and come down when you're finished. The midday meal is nearly ready."

"*Ach*, it's a lovely room." Angela walked to the window. "Such a pretty view from here."

Emma looked out the window. "I know. I should appreciate it more, but there always seems so much to do and so little time."

"I'll help you while I'm here. You just tell me what you'd like me to do," Angela said.

Emma smiled. "There's not much to do today. Are you hungry?"

"A little hungry."

"Leave the unpacking then, and we'll have the meal now."

They made their way downstairs. Emma had already prepared most of the meal ahead of time and only had to heat a couple of things on the stove. "Cup of meadow tea?" Emma asked.

"*Jah*. Let me get it," Angela said.

Emma showed Angela around the kitchen, so she knew where everything was kept. Moments later they sat at the kitchen table sipping hot tea.

"Elsa-May tells me that you're to meet Robert Geiger soon."

Angela pulled a face. "I'm a little nervous. He's arranged for me to meet him tomorrow. He's even sent me money to get a taxi from here."

"I could've driven you."

Angela gave a high-pitched giggle. "It'd make me more nervous if someone else was there. What if we didn't like each other at all? Then things would be really awkward."

"I suppose so. Has he told you all about himself?" Emma asked.

"He told me he's got his *bruder's* son, Jacob, living with him. He said that he's a very smart boy."

"I've heard Jacob can be a little bit of a handful."

"What do you mean, Emma?"

"*Ach,* nothing to worry about, I'm sure. You heard of how Jacob's parents died?"

"In a buggy accident, wasn't it?" Angela asked.

Emma nodded. "Unfortunate circumstances. Jacob's *daed* was Robert's *bruder*. I'd say Robert hasn't married up until now because he's been too involved with looking after Jacob."

"*Jah,* that's what his letters as *gut* as said. It must be awful for Jacob. He's blessed his uncle took him in. From his letters I can tell that Robert adores him."

"You're going to visit Robert tomorrow then?"

"*Jah,* I've got his address. Elsa-May said it's not too far from here."

"Not far at all," Emma said.

Angela leaned forward. "Is there anything you can tell me about Robert?"

Emma thought for a while. "*Nee,* I don't know him well enough."

Angela took a deep breath. "That's all right. I guess I'll just have to see for myself."

Emma could imagine how nervous Angela would be after months of writing to a man and now finally about to meet him.

CHAPTER 4

*Because strait is the gate, and narrow is the way, which leadeth
unto life, and few there be that find it.*
Matthew 7:14

ANGELA SAT with Robert and tried to get over the shock of
Jacob being the one to write the letters. Despite the shock,
she did feel a little more comfortable than when she had
first arrived.

"It was my *Ant* Elsa-May who suggested I write you."
Angela felt the need to explain that to him, since he hadn't
had the benefit of reading any of her letters.

Robert smiled. "I recall she did try to tell me of
someone who might suit me, on more than one occasion.
I did try to tell her about the boy and how it complicates
things for me."

Angela did not quite know why he thought he could

not be married because of Jacob. Jacob had said himself that he wanted Robert to have a *fraa*.

"I heard you took Jacob in when his *mudder* and *vadder* were killed in a buggy accident."

Robert stared straight ahead and took a mouthful of tea. "Jacob's *daed* was my *bruder*, Ross. What you might not have heard was that my *bruder* had been charged with murder and was out on bail when he and Jacob's *mudder* were killed in the accident."

"*Nee*, I didn't know about that."

"I've been trying to clear Ross' name for the sake of the boy. That's what Ross would've wanted."

"Does Jacob know that his *vadder* was accused of such a thing?"

Robert shook his head. "If he's heard things here and there, he hasn't mentioned anything to me."

"How far have you gotten trying to clear his name?" Angela asked.

"Not very far. I've got small pieces of information and that's all."

"Elsa-May's had some success with things like this in the past. Have you considered getting her help with it?"

Robert tipped his head back and laughed. "Dear old Elsa-May being of help in a matter like this?"

"It might seem unlikely, but it's true. Elsa-May and her *schweschder*, Ettie, have had success; they even know detectives. In fact, one of their nephews is a detective."

Robert drummed his fingers on the long, wooden kitchen table. "Really?"

Angela nodded enthusiastically.

"Your coming here might be an answer to prayer, Miss Bontreger."

Angela's heart beat faster when he looked at her. He was a handsome man and even more so when he smiled. She had been waiting on a time like this, a time where *Gott's* favor would shine upon her.

Robert was silent as he slowly raised the hot tea to his lips. He took a mouthful, placed the cup carefully onto the table and looked once more into Angela's eyes. "Write a *gut* letter, did I?"

Angela smiled. "I'm here, aren't I?"

Angela and Robert laughed, which eased any leftover tension between them.

"I'm staying at Emma Kurtzler's *haus*, and Elsa-May and Ettie are coming for dinner tonight. Why don't you tell me everything you know and I'll pass it on to Elsa-May and see what she makes of it?"

Robert ran his fingers over his chin. "Wouldn't hurt, I guess. I kept in contact with the police for a time, but I think they came to see me as a pest at some point. They'll hardly speak to me now when I go in there. They certainly don't listen to anything I have to say. I've given them new information, but I think they don't want to put any effort into the case. They appear to be happy to leave things as they are. Every time I've been to there to talk to one of the police, I've overhead at least one of them grumbling about paperwork. I came to realize that all they want to do is drink coffee and eat donuts."

Angela smiled at his comment. "They're not all like that."

Robert rubbed his right eyebrow and then looked back

at Angela. "Why don't I take you back to Emma's *haus* and I'll tell you everything on the way?"

"*Jah, denke.*"

Robert leaned his body back slightly. "Forgive me. I've put you in an awkward position. You came here expecting something quite different and now I'm saddling you with all my burdens."

Angela instinctively put her hand on his arm. "*Nee*, not at all. I'm happy to be of help."

Robert sat up straight, put his fingers lightly on her hand and stared into her eyes. Angela pulled her hand away and looked down. She wanted to keep her hand there, but she did not want him to think that she was anxiously looking for a husband. The last thing she wanted was to appear to Robert as though she were desperate.

"I'm sorry, Angela. I'm not used to a woman's soft hands against my skin."

Angela smiled and kept her gaze away from him. "Robert, you must stop apologizing to me; it's not necessary." Angela could scarcely breathe as she felt his gaze upon her. She stood up. "Should we go now?"

"Visit me tomorrow? I mean, to tell me what Elsa-May makes of the whole thing?"

"*Jah*, I will."

Before Angela could say more, Robert called out to Jacob who was still in his bedroom. "I'm going out now, Jacob. You can come out of your room. I'll be back later. I'll tell you of your punishment when I return." He turned to Angela. "Let's go." He walked out the door toward the barn with Angela hurrying behind him.

Angela leaned against the barn door and watched Robert as he hitched a buggy to one of his horses. She scrutinized his strong arms lift the buggy and strap the leather onto the horse. He spoke to the horse in a low, soothing voice as he worked. Angela liked people who were kind to animals.

Elsa-May was right; this could be the mann for me, she thought. *We both felt something as we sat in the kitchen just now; I'm sure he felt it too. His touch sent tingles right through me; surely that means something.*

During the ride home, Robert told Angela everything he knew about his *bruder's* case wherein he was falsely accused of murder. Angela wrote everything down so she wouldn't forget anything.

CHAPTER 5

A hot-tempered man stirs up strife, but he who is slow to anger quiets contention.
Proverbs 15:18

THAT EVENING, not only did Elsa-May and Ettie come to Emma's *haus* for dinner, Silvie and Maureen came as well.

Angela was well aware of her *Ant* Elsa-May's crime solving abilities and she guessed that these widows helped her.

As the ladies were all helping to prepare the meal, Elsa-May pulled Angela aside for a quiet word. "How did you like Robert?"

"*Ach*, it was terrible. It wasn't he who wrote the letters; it was Jacob."

"His nephew, little Jacob?"

"Yeah, he's most likely eleven or twelve. He admitted

to it and he said he wanted his *onkel* to be happy. I still find it hard to believe that I was fooled by a child of his age. It's obvious that he is a very smart boy."

Elsa-May chuckled. "Bless his little soul."

"I was extremely embarrassed. I felt such a fool going there to meet someone I thought I might marry and he knew nothing of me, nothing at all."

Elsa-May waved her hand dismissively. "Apart from all that, what did you think of Robert?"

Angela giggled a little. "He was lovely. Just the sort of *mann* I'd like. You were right about that, *Ant*."

Elsa-May leaned toward her and spoke quietly. "Don't give up; *Gott* works in mysterious ways."

"Did you know about his *bruder,* Jacob's *daed*?" Angela asked.

"*Ach, jah.* A terrible business, on bail for murder and then killed before he could clear his name. Both Ross and his *fraa*, Linda, died in that buggy accident."

"So, you believe he was innocent?" Angela's eyes grew wide.

Elsa-May filled her cheeks with air. "I don't know any details. I've always assumed he was innocent. No Amish *mann* would ever have done what he was accused of."

"Robert wants to clear his *bruder's* name for Jacob's sake. He thinks that's why Jacob has been unruly. Although, he's not sure whether Jacob knows or not, but he must have heard some kind of gossip. Anyway, I said I'd get your help."

Elsa-May nodded slowly. "*Jah*, I'll help. We'll all help. Did he tell you anything?"

"He told me everything he knows and I even wrote it down."

Elsa-May patted her on the arm. "Tell the ladies over dinner."

Angela drew her chin backwards. "*Ant*, that's not very nice dinner conversation for the ladies."

Elsa-May held Angela's arm firmly. "Believe me, they'll appreciate the conversation more than talking about the last quilt they sewed or the batch of strawberry preserves they've just bottled."

Once the dinner table was set, they all sat down to eat.

Elsa-May began. "Now ladies, you all know Robert Geiger and how his *bruder*, Ross Geiger, was accused of murder before he died in the buggy accident?"

The ladies nodded.

"We are going to try and clear his name," Elsa-May said.

"What if he's guilty?" Ettie said.

Elsa-May glared at her *schweschder*. "Then things remain the same, but if he's innocent, we will be able to clear his name for his son's sake." She looked at all the widows. "All in?"

"*Jah*," the widows chimed.

"Tell us what you know, Angela." Elsa-May said.

"This is what Robert told me. Two years ago a man was found dead, tied to a wooden cross. He was found by a couple of children on their way to *skul*. A witness came forward and said that she saw Ross hitting the man on the head with a rock and she saw him tie him to the cross. It was the woman's testimony that had him arrested, even though Ross' *fraa* said that he had been home all evening.

SAMANTHA PRICE

The police believed that it was an Amish person because of the religious implications of the murder, with the cross and all."

"Who was the man who was killed?" Maureen asked.

Angela shrugged her shoulders. "I don't know. Robert says that no one knows."

"How did Ross get bail if he was charged with murder?" Emma asked.

Ettie said, "From what I remember of the case, they did not think he was a flight risk since he had no passport and did not know anyone outside of the community."

"Is that all you know, Angela?" Elsa-May asked.

"*Jah*, that's all I know. I'm seeing Robert again tomorrow. Is there anything I should ask him?"

The widows looked at each other.

"*Nee*, that's all we need for now until we think of some questions," Elsa-May said.

Ettie said, "Elsa-May, you'll have to go and ask Crowley some questions."

"Indeed." Elsa-May nodded. Detective Crowley had been a source of information to them in the past and was always more than willing to help. Although, not everyone liked Detective Crowley even if he was helpful.

"Better you than me." When everyone looked at her, Emma said. "He always makes me feel guilty and uncomfortable."

Ettie pointed a long, bony finger at Emma. "He always helps us."

Emma nodded and put her head down and wished that she hadn't spoken at all. She knew Ettie was right.

Silvie said, "What's the plan, Elsa-May?"

Elsa-May placed her knife and fork down and swallowed the chicken she had been chewing on. "Let's see now. I'll visit Crowley to find out what he can tell me about the case. That's really all we can do until we have more information. I'll go first thing in the morning."

Angela turned to Emma. "I hope you didn't mind having this conversation over dinner, Emma."

"*Nee*, not at all. Everyone here has had a little experience in these matters. We're all happy to help in whatever way we can."

"You came here to see Robert?" Silvie asked.

Angela's face flushed scarlet. "I suppose it doesn't matter if everyone at this table knows. Elsa-May had me write to Robert, but it appears my first letter was intercepted by his nephew, Jacob." Angela put her fingertips to her forehead and continued, "Jacob wrote back to me and he's been writing to me ever since, pretending to be his *onkel*. Both Robert and I only just found out today."

Maureen giggled. "*Ach*, that little - naughty boy."

Silvie asked, "So what's the plan, Elsa-May, where do we start?

"Ettie, you go visiting people and see what you can find out. People like to talk to you."

"Okay," Ettie said. "I'll start visiting tomorrow and ask a lot of questions."

"Emma, you go and visit Crowley," Elsa-May said.

"Me? Why do I have to visit Crowley? Didn't you say you were going to do it, Elsa-May? You're the one he respects. I told you he makes me feel uncomfortable and guilty all the time."

"Just do it, Emma. The rest of us will spread out, visit

people and ask questions without appearing obvious. Everyone in the community should recall the incident. We have to find out who the witness was and who the dead man was."

"You're going back to Robert's place tomorrow aren't you, Angela?"

"*Jah*, I am. In the afternoon," Angela said.

"Ask questions about the witness and the dead man. Find out if Robert knows anything about them and find out what other little things he might have forgotten to mention."

Angela nodded. "I will."

"Now, if we're all done with that business, we've got dessert," Emma said.

Angela looked up to see Emma and Maureen carrying desserts to the table. There was a tall chocolate cake with pink and white marshmallows on top, chocolate slices, ice-cream and round chocolate balls covered with coconut.

"Someone likes chocolate," Angela said with a laugh.

"Chocolate is a weakness of mine," Emma said as she sat down.

Maureen took a large knife and cut the tall chocolate cake into slices. "I hope no one here is watching what they eat."

"Not anymore," Ettie said.

After a large meal and an even larger dessert, the widows went home.

"I'll dry the dishes, Emma. That way we can talk," Angela said.

"*Denke*. How are you liking Lancaster County so far?"

"Everyone seems really friendly. I like the countryside; it's quite similar to back home."

"I heard you tell Elsa-May that you like Robert," Emma said.

"*Jah*. I don't know what he thinks of me. A strange lady showing up at his *haus* expecting that he should know of me. It was the most embarrassing moment of my life."

"He's a *gut* man, from what I know of him. He would have felt bad when he found out what Jacob had done."

Angela looked thoughtful. "He did."

"Seems to me as though Robert is always sad or distracted by something. Now I know more of what happened to his *bruder*, it all makes sense. Mind you I didn't know the Geigers that well."

"I appreciate you letting me stay here, Emma."

"You're doing me a favor. I like having company. I told Elsa-May you are welcome to stay as long as you want." Emma took the opportunity to try and find out more about the cases Elsa-May had worked on in the past. Emma was involved in the Pluver case and the more recent murder of old Frank, but she knew that Elsa-May and Ettie had worked on many more cases with Detective Crowley. "You're aware then of Elsa-May working on similar cases to try and solve them, and such?"

"*Jah*, someone was murdered once, down my way, and Elsa-May helped with that," Angela said.

A smile spread across Emma's face. "I see. I knew she'd done these things before."

"Don't tell her I told you; she's very secretive about these things. I don't want her to be cross with me."

"I won't tell," Emma said.

"My *daed* used to say that Elsa-May's every bit as smart as a *mann*."

Emma raised her eyebrows and bit her tongue to avoid making a comment, although she couldn't help but say, "I guess your *daed* would see that as a compliment."

"Very much so." Angela laughed. "I guess he thinks that *menner* have to be smarter."

Emma vigorously scrubbed a saucepan. "Women are just as smart, I'm sure."

"Elsa-May said you might be married soon?"

"*Jah*, to Wil Jacobson. He lives next door. You met him yesterday, didn't you?"

"*Nee*, I didn't meet anyone," Angela said.

"That's right; he left just before you arrived. Your taxi passed him just as he was leaving my *haus*."

"That's right, I do remember passing a buggy that looked as though it was coming from your place. Is he nice?"

"He is. I'm blessed to have had two *gut menner* in my life. Why have you never married before now, Angela?"

"Where I come from isn't like here. There's not many *menner* to choose from and they get snapped up pretty quickly. I'm quieter than the other girls so it made things that much harder for me. The other girls can talk to the boys easily. I never had any *bruders,* so I'm not used to boys. There was one boy I liked once." Angela rubbed her neck. "I was too nervous to speak to the boys especially the ones I liked. Anyway, before too long, they were all married."

"That's the disadvantage of a small community, I suppose."

"My *Ant* Elsa-May's been telling me about Robert for a long time. I finally gave in and wrote to him and well… you know the rest."

Emma put the last saucepan in the cupboard and wiped down her long, wooden table in the kitchen. "All done; just a quick sweep with the broom and we can sit down."

"Let me do it, Emma." Angela rushed for the broom and began to sweep the kitchen.

"*Denke*, I'll make us some meadow tea." Emma put the kettle on the stove and got the tea ready. "Don't fuss too much with the floor, Angela. I'll wash it tomorrow."

Once the tea was poured, Emma carried the tea, chocolate cookies and her favorite chocolate soft centers out to the living room.

"This is a nice big room, Emma," Angela said as she sat on the couch.

"*Jah*, it's just as we wanted. Levi, my late husband built the *haus* for us." Emma passed Angela the tea.

"Will you live in Wil's *haus* when you get married?"

Emma sat down opposite Angela and put the pink flowered teacup to her lips and took a sip. The teacups had been a gift from Levi on the announcement of their marriage. They were far more fancy than the china she had been used to, which was plain white with maybe a small pattern. As she placed the cup down onto the saucer, she said, "We haven't even decided that." Emma looked around the room. "This *haus* reminds me of Levi. I wouldn't want someone else to live in it, neither would I feel comfortable living in it with Wil, especially when he has his own *haus* on the next door farm."

Emma watched Angela bite into a chocolate cookie.

"You know, now I say that out aloud I realize that's what's stopping Wil and I moving forward. I just can't see where we could live," Emma said.

"That makes sense."

"Does it? Sometimes it seems as nothing makes sense to me. Nothing has fallen into place. Nowhere feels right for us to live."

"Perhaps you're thinking ahead too much? I know it would be hard to leave this place, but it is after all just a *haus*," Angela said.

Nee, it's not just a haus, Emma thought. Emma drew comfort from living in the *haus* that Levi had built for them. It was as if part of him was still there. Angela's words seemed harsh. Emma studied Angela as she sat in front of her, nibbling on the cookie. She hadn't meant any offence; Angela couldn't know the feelings that she had for the *haus* or the comfort it filled her with.

Angela looked up and caught her eye. "I didn't mean to upset you, Emma."

"I'm not upset. I'm realizing just how attached I am to this *haus*."

Angela nodded sympathetically and passed her up the plate of cookies. Emma took a cookie and held it in her hand. What was the answer? Where would she and Wil live after they married?

Angela broke through Emma's pondering when she said, "Robert asked me to go back there tomorrow."

Emma was pleased that they had arranged to meet again. "I'll drive you there."

"*Denke*, would afternoon suit you? He's hoping I'll have

some word from Elsa-May helping to clear his *bruder's* name. I'm hoping we might have some information by afternoon."

Emma raised her eyebrows. "That seems a little hopeful since he's gone two years with no information."

Angela gasped and covered her mouth. "I hope I didn't give him false hope when I told him of Elsa-May's abilities."

"We'll all do the best that we can. Besides, it'll give you reason to keep speaking to him." Emma giggled.

"*Jah*, I know it will."

"I saw when he brought you here this afternoon that he had the look in his eye that a *mann* has when he likes what he sees."

Angela's face brightened. "You think so?"

Emma smiled at the look of delight on Angela's face. "I do."

Angela breathed in and let her breath out slowly. "I'll sleep well tonight."

00079004379

Sell your books at
sellbackyourBook.com!
Go to sellbackyourBook.com
and get an instant price quote.
We even pay the shipping - see
what your old books are worth
today!

CHAPTER 6

But without faith it is impossible to please him: for he that cometh to God must believe that he is, and that he is a rewarder of them that diligently seek him.
Hebrews 11:6

EMMA WAS WOKEN by a shaft of light entering her bedroom from where her two curtains met in the middle. She had forgotten to close the gap the night before. She always woke at the slightest light. Most nights before she went to bed, she would adjust her curtains so they would blanket the morning light. Too late – she was already wide-awake.

As she stretched her hands over her head, she recalled that today she had been designated by Elsa-May to visit her very least favorite detective. She had to go that morning because she had told Angela she would drive her to Robert's *haus* in the afternoon. Emma got out of bed and hurried to get her chores done so she could make an early start, figuring that Crowley would get into his office at around nine.

The morning hours passed quickly for Emma and now she stood outside Detective Crowley's office, knocking tentatively on his door.

"Come in," Crowley said.

She stepped through the doorway and he rose to his feet when he saw her. "Mrs. Jacobson?"

"*Nee*, it's Mrs. Kurtzler."

"Yes, of course, I was getting confused with Wil Jacobson. So you haven't married Mr. Jacobson yet?"

Did the detective know that she was conflicted over the prospect of marrying Wil so soon after Levi died? Could he possibly be that good of a detective?

"Detective, with all due respect, I did not come here to discuss my marital status." Emma silently reprimanded herself; she knew that was a silly thing to say if she was to keep him on side. But he seemed to have a way of getting under her skin. Why would he call her Mrs. Jacobson? He knew her name very well and Emma knew for sure and for certain that he had an excellent memory.

A smile softened the detective's sharp features. "Have a seat." He motioned to the chair in front of his desk.

They sat at the same time.

"What brings you here then, if it's not to discuss your marital status?"

Keep calm, he's trying to bait you again, Emma cautioned herself. "Elsa-May sent me." Emma knew that the detective respected Elsa-May, so she congratulated herself on thinking to use her name.

The detective leaned forward. "I'm listening."

"Do you remember a case some years ago involving an Amish man called Ross Geiger?"

"I do. Strange case that one. The body was tied to a cross."

"That's the one," Emma said pleased that he remembered it.

"What of it?"

"Elsa-May sent me to ask you who the witness was and who the dead man was."

The detective rubbed his left ear. "I recall the accused man died in a buggy accident shortly after he was granted bail."

"Yes, he and his wife, before he could clear his name. Before proper investigations could take place."

The detective bit on the end of a pencil. "So, that's what this is about? Elsa-May is looking to clear his name?"

Emma nodded. "Were you working on the case?"

"No, but I knew about it. It should all be on the computer." The detective turned his attention to the computer on his desk. He pressed a button and tilted the screen to face him. After a few moments and a few clicks, the detective asked, "How long ago? What was the accused's name again?"

"Roughly two years ago and his name was Ross Geiger."

"Got it. Here we go. The dead man was never identified, but we do have his DNA records, dental records, body measurements and fingerprints. He did not fit the description of any missing person at the time or since." The detective looked at Emma. "The dead man had no criminal history because his fingerprints weren't in our database."

Emma nodded. "Does it give a description of him?"

The detective turned back to the computer screen. "Five foot ten inches, light brown hair, brown eyes and no identifying marks or scars. He was wearing dark blue jeans, brown leather boots and a blue shirt with a collar."

"What does it say about the witness?" Emma asked.

"Mrs. Kurtzler, you know I can't give you sensitive information like that. But, if you should happen to over-hear me talking to myself as I'm looking at the computer, then I wouldn't be breaking any rules." The detective looked again, at the computer screen. "The witness was, or I should say is, Juliana Redcliffe." The detective was quiet for a moment as he read the information. "She said she couldn't sleep that night and went for a walk down by the river. She heard a noise and looked through the undergrowth to see Ross Geiger hit the man in the head with a large stone several times then he tied him to a wooden cross."

"Does that sound odd to you, Detective? That someone would go for a walk alone in the woods if they can't sleep? Do people do that? Especially a woman alone at night?" Emma asked.

"Sounds odd, but how is someone to say that she didn't go for a walk?" The detective kept his eyes fixed on the screen. "It happened two miles away from Ross

Geiger's house and five hundred meters from the witness' house."

"And where's that?"

The detective lowered his head and looked up at Emma, and said, "What?"

"The witness' house."

The detective leaned back in his chair. "This is a murder. Only a trained professional should stick their nose in."

Emma stared back at the detective and held his gaze for some time.

"All right, I'll speak to her today. If she still lives there," the detective said.

Emma wriggled in the chair. "Could you possibly do it this morning?"

The detective cocked his head to the side and frowned. "It's an old case. What's the rush?"

"Well, you see. We really want to clear Ross Geiger's name for his son. He's becoming a handful to look after and Ross's *bruder* is taking care of him and Angela, who's staying at my place, was writing letters to…"

"Spare me the finer details, I'm sure they're very interesting – to someone." He looked back at the computer. "Yes, we have Robert Geiger's details here, on file. It would appear he's been to see us several times." The detective stood up. "I'll talk to the witness and then come to see you. Do you still live at the same place?"

"*Jah*, still the same *haus*."

As Emma was walking out of his office the detective called after her. "Mrs. Kurtzler."

She turned to face him. "Please, call me Emma."

The detective smiled. "Do you still have that fat cat?"

Emma smiled at the thought of Growler. "Yes, I've still got Growler. He's part of the *familye* now."

A look of amusement crossed the detective's hard face. It was the detective who suggested that Emma take Growler to live with her after his owner had been murdered. At the time Emma hardly had a choice, it was take Growler or the detective was going to have him put to sleep. Or was he? That's what the detective said that he would do at the time. She remembered distinctly that the detective said that he'd call animal welfare and have the cat put to sleep if she didn't take him. Was he bluffing? He seemed interested in Growler's welfare. Emma shook her head. She'd never know what went on in the detective's head.

CHAPTER 7

Let us come before his presence with thanksgiving, and make a
joyful noise unto him with psalms.
Psalms 95:2

EMMA DROVE her buggy back home, pleased with the fact that Crowley was going to question the witness. It was still early in the day and Emma knew that Angela would not expect her back for some time, so Emma pulled up her buggy outside Wil's front door. Wil came out to meet her.

"Emma, I was just about to put some *kaffe* on."

"Lovely, I'll have one, *denke*."

"You sit here and I'll put the hot water on to boil."

Emma sat on the white porch chair and looked out across Wil's farm. What a coincidence it was that they both owned farms adjacent to one another. He'd been a *gut* friend to her late husband and she knew without a doubt that Levi would whole-heartedly approve of the two of them getting married.

Wil fell into the seat next to her. "What's on your mind, Emma? I can tell something is."

Emma smiled. Wil could read her like a book. "You still want to get married next wedding season, don't you?"

"Or as soon as the bishop can marry us and as soon as you are willing."

"It occurred to me that I've been hesitating because of my *haus.* Because it was the house Levi built for us to live in." Emma studied Wil's face and noticed that he did not look happy. "Wil, don't be like that. I need to speak to you about these things. I want to be able to tell you all things that trouble me."

"*Jah*, Emma, we need to discuss these things. I know that. I didn't realize how you felt about the *haus*."

"I don't know what to do about the *haus*. I mean, where do you see us living?" Emma nibbled on the end of her fingernail. She had nearly beaten the habit, but every now and again she realized she was chewing her nails.

Wil turned his body toward her a little more. "I always thought that we'd live here in my *haus*. It's plenty big enough and I'll change it to whatever suits you. I can make the kitchen bigger and better. Did you have other ideas?"

Emma shook her head slowly. "*Nee,* I guess it's either my *haus* or your *haus*."

"I wouldn't feel right living in another *mann's* house even though Levi was like my own *bruder*." Wil picked up Emma's hand. "Emma, if it means that much to you I'll be happy living anywhere as long as I'm with you. It doesn't matter."

"*Denke*, Wil. We don't have to decide now, do we?"

"*Nee*, don't upset yourself. We've got time to decide, a few months anyway."

Emma smiled and was pleased that she could bring up the subject of the *haus* even though she knew it would remind Wil that she was once married to another *mann.*

She left Wil sitting on his porch and drove her buggy the short distance to her *haus.* Emma knew she should be sewing for her wedding and planning things as she had with her first wedding. With her first wedding, she took pleasure in every stitch she sewed in her special linen dress. Now her second wedding was approaching, she knew that the marriage was the important part and not just the wedding day. Besides, she knew she could get all the sewing and organizing done in a very short space of time; she'd only need weeks before the wedding.

Angela was sweeping the porch when Emma pulled the buggy up. "*Denke,* Angela. You're my guest you don't have to do anything."

"Idle hands and minds are the devil's playground, my *mudder* always said." Angela smiled as she leaned on the broom. "I prefer to stay busy."

"I'll fix the horse up and then I'll come inside and tell you what I found out from Detective Crowley."

Since it was nearing the middle of the day, they sat out on the porch to eat the midday meal. They ate chicken and coleslaw while Emma told Angela all the information that the detective gave her.

"*Denke* for all you've done, Emma."

"I always get nervous speaking to the detective. He did tell me all he could which surprised me. He said he's coming straight here once he talks to the witness. I hope she still lives around these parts."

"*Jah*, I hope so too."

"I suppose you could take the buggy rather than have me drive you to Robert's *haus*. I didn't think of that earlier. I don't have to go anywhere else today, so you're welcome to use it." Emma said.

"*Denke*, Emma that's kind of you."

They both looked up the road when they heard the car coming toward them. It was a police car and Detective Crowley was being driven by a uniformed police officer.

"I don't know why he never drives himself," Emma whispered to Angela. "He always has someone drive him in a police car."

"Doesn't that defeat the purpose of wearing plain clothes?" Angela said.

Both girls giggled, but quickly regained their composure when the detective leaped out of the car and headed toward them.

"Good afternoon, ladies."

Both ladies rose to their feet and Emma said, "Afternoon, Detective. This is Angela Bontreger."

The detective nodded his head to Angela.

"Angela was the one who told me of the... the whole thing that I spoke to you about this morning. Come inside."

Once the three of them were seated around the table the detective said, "It's highly unusual to discuss these

48

things with civilians. I'm only doing it because Elsa-May sent you, Emma. Elsa-May's helped me in the past."

"I appreciate that. What did you find out? Does the witness still live at the same place?" Emma asked.

The two girls leaned slightly forward to hear what the detective had to say.

"Yes she's living at the same place. What's more, she's sticking to her story. She went for a walk that night and saw the Amish man hit the deceased in the head several times with a rock. Then she watched from a distance as he tied him to a wooden cross."

Emma glanced at Angela and noticed that her face had turned pale. She patted Angela on the arm. At least Emma had heard these kinds of things before, but Angela was new to them.

"Detective, if it was dark how could she see or properly identify the person who did it?" Angela asked.

"She picked him out of a lineup. She is still sure that Ross Geiger is the man she saw commit the crime."

"Is there any new information at all?" Emma asked.

The detective shook his head. "What I can do is run the DNA again and see if any new matches are available; a lot can change in two or more years."

"In what way?" Angela asked.

"More and more DNA samples are being done and recorded on the FBI database. There's a chance we may find a match. With no more evidence and the witness sticking to her story, that's the only avenue we can go down at this stage."

Emma rubbed her chin. "Does the witness have any

link to the man who was murdered, or any link at all to Ross?"

"She says no, but I'll see what I can find out." The detective looked at his watch. "I'd better get going."

"Thank you, Detective. I appreciate you following up on the matter," Emma said.

The detective smiled and said goodbye to the two ladies before he got back in the police car.

"Doesn't seem like we've got much to go on," Emma said.

"Seems odd that the witness was able to say without a doubt that Ross was the man she saw," Angela said.

Emma caught herself before she put fingers to her mouth. "*Jah*, and that was enough to have him arrested. And how would she be able to know for sure in the dark? Elsa-May and Ettie will be here soon. They might have uncovered something from all the people they've spoken with this morning."

Angela smiled and nodded. "I'm having an exciting change here in Lancaster County. At home I'd be doing the same old thing that I do day after day. Is it always like this?"

Emma giggled. "It never was like this until I became friends with the other widows. Something exciting is always happening now. Maureen was a *gut* friend of mine and when Levi died, she brought me into her little group of widows with Silvie and the others."

An hour later, Elsa-May and Ettie arrived at Emma's *haus*. Elsa-May nearly ran into Emma's *haus*, leaving Ettie to tie up the horse.

Elsa-May threw herself down on Emma's couch.

"Well, we've found something out. We spoke to Bob Pluver's *mudder*; she knew Ross and Linda Geiger quite well it seems. Before they died, she was visiting them and they told her that the woman who told the police that Ross was guilty was living with the man who died.

"How did they know?" Emma asked.

"Rumors and talk, the man had been living with the woman for weeks. That's what's rumored anyway," Elsa-May said.

"How can that be? The police don't even know that. Wouldn't that have come up in their investigations?" Emma asked.

Ettie came through the door at that moment. "Did Elsa-May tell you that the witness knew the man who was killed?"

Emma turned to Ettie. "*Jah*, she did. Wouldn't that information alone be enough to clear Ross's name?"

"It should be, if it's true. Let's see what else we can piece together. You got any of those chocolate chip cookies, Emma?" Elsa-May asked.

"*Jah*, I've always got chocolate chip cookies." Emma went to the kitchen to get the cookies and called out from the kitchen, "I'll brew some tea. Don't talk about anything important 'til I come back."

Ettie came into the kitchen to help Emma. They fixed a large tray with tea, cookies and cakes to take into the living room.

As Emma set the tray down on a small table in the living room, she said, "*Ach*, have you two had lunch yet? I could fix you something."

"*Nee*, this will be fine for us," Ettie said.

Elsa-May said, "*Jah*, I was getting a little weak. This will pick me up."

Elsa-May was a larger lady, but Emma wasn't too worried about them going without food because she knew that everywhere they had visited that morning would have offered them food. Amish folk never like to see anyone go hungry and there's always plenty of food, if not on the stove then in the cold box.

"Wait a minute, the police don't know the identity of the man who was murdered. Did you speak to someone who knew who he was?" Emma asked.

"It seems as though he was, according to Mrs. Pluver, living with the woman who gave testimony against Ross Geiger for the murder, but no one seems to know his name or anything about him at all."

"What does this all mean in plain English?" Angela asked.

"It means, what I said before," Elsa-May's tone was slightly annoyed with Angela not being able to keep up with the information. "The man who was murdered was living with the witness and she said that she saw Ross kill the man and spoke nothing to the police of knowing the man personally."

Ettie said, "Seems pretty sketchy to me."

"I have to go and tell Robert what I've found out this afternoon," Angela said.

Elsa-May put her hand up. "*Nee*, tell him nothing. Not 'til we've figured it out. We don't want him to jump to conclusions and get in the way of things."

"What am I to say to him then?" Angela said with her fingers to her mouth.

"Tell him that we haven't been able to find anything out yet, then flirt with him," Ettie said, which caused Angela to giggle.

"I'll hitch the buggy for you now, Angela. That way you can have more time with him before it gets dark." Emma headed to the barn to hitch the buggy then led the horse to the front of the *haus*.

Angela climbed in the buggy. "*Denke*, Emma. Are you sure you don't need the buggy for the rest of the day?"

"*Nee*, you go on and enjoy yourself. Do you remember which way to go?"

"*Jah*," Angela said.

The three widows watched Angela drive the buggy down the dirt packed driveway.

CHAPTER 8

I have come as a light into the world, that whoever believes in Me should not abide in darkness.
John 12:46

As Angela approached Robert's *haus,* her heart began to pound. She hoped that he felt the attraction for her that she felt for him. She stopped her horse just past the *haus* in front of the barn.

"You looking for *Onkel* Robert?"

Angela looked to the direction of the voice and saw Jacob in a nearby field. "*Jah.* Hello, Jacob."

"He said to tell you he'd be back soon. He wasn't sure what time you'd be coming and he had to go into town for some supplies."

When Angela got down from the buggy, Jacob said, "I'll fix your horse."

"*Denke*, Jacob."

Angela watched Jacob as he unhitched the horse, rubbed him down and set him into the paddock adjacent to the barn. "That's very kind of you."

"There's fresh water in there for him. I just filled the trough. I can make you tea if you'd like some?"

Angela nodded. "That'll be lovely. I wouldn't mind a cup of meadow tea."

"Follow me."

"Do you want me to help you with the tea?" Angela asked.

"*Nee*, I make tea for *Onkel* all the time. Sit down here." Jacob pulled out a chair from the kitchen table.

As Angela sat, she wondered what she should say to Jacob. She was nearly going to ask him how long he'd lived with his *onkel*, but considered that might bring back memories of his parents' accident. "So, you like *skul*?"

"*Jah*, I like it *gut* enough."

"What do you think you'd like to do when you grow up?"

Jacob poured the hot water into two cups. "I'd like to be a pilot like my *daed*."

"What? You mean, fly planes and such?"

"*Jah*, someone said that's what my real *daed* did."

"Your real *daed*?" Angela put her head to the side. "Wasn't Ross Geiger your real *daed*?"

Jacob shook his head. "I was adopted."

Angela was a little shocked, but tried not to show it. "You were? I didn't know. Do many people know that you were adopted?"

He set a cup of tea in front of Angela. "Just my *onkel* I

guess, maybe the bishop, I s'pose. And my real *daed's schweschder,* my *ant.* She's an *Englischer* too."

"To be a pilot means your real, I mean, your biological *daed* was an *Englisher?*" Angela hoped that she wasn't crossing the line talking to Jacob about his birth parents without Robert there. It seemed that Jacob was quite open with the information about his adoption.

"*Jah,* and I'm going to leave the community as soon as I'm old enough and I'm going to get my pilot's license and *Onkel* Robert won't be able to stop me."

"Do you know much about your *daed,* the pilot?"

"His *schweschder* told me that he died, some time ago."

"I'm so sorry to hear that."

Jacob pulled a plate of cookies out of the cupboard and placed them on the table. "*Onkel* says that death and life are just a cycle and we shouldn't be sad about something that *Gott* has set into place."

"What about your biological *mamm?*"

"I don't know about her; my *ant* wouldn't tell me about her. She said that the least said, soonest mended." Jacob sat next to her. "I'm sorry that I wrote to you pretending to be *Onkel* Robert."

"I accepted your apology yesterday, Jacob. Don't concern yourself, all is forgiven from my part."

"I know it was wrong and I felt bad about doing it. I just wanted *Onkel* to be happy." Jacob smiled at Angela. "I think you'd make him a *gut fraa.*"

Angela smiled back at Jacob. "*Denke.*"

They both lifted their heads to the sound of hoof beats.

"Sounds like it might be your *onkel* home," Angela said.

Jacob ran to the front door and Angela stood behind him.

"I'll fix the horse, *Onkel*." Jacob ran to take the reins from Robert.

Robert walked past Jacob and playfully messed his hair with his large hand. "*Denke*, Jacob." Robert looked up at Angela, who was standing just inside the front door. "I'm sorry I wasn't here when you arrived. We didn't arrange a firm time so I took the opportunity to go and buy something nice for us to eat." He looked over at Jacob. "He's been taking care of you by the looks?" Robert asked.

"*Jah*, he looked after the horse, then he fixed me a cup of tea."

"Come along. A cup of tea sounds *gut*." Robert led the way back into the kitchen and made himself a cup of tea. "He's a *gut* boy most of the time." Robert placed a package on the table then sat down. "I bought some cupcakes for us."

"*Ach*, I love cupcakes."

"Who doesn't love cupcakes? I know Jacob does. We have them on special occasions." Robert looked out the kitchen window. "He's still fooling around with the horses."

"He must be a *gut* help to you."

Robert took the lid off the package of cupcakes. "*Jah*, he is. He loves the horses. I didn't punish him. I gave him a stern talking to and he saw the error of his ways. As you said, his heart was in the right place."

"I'm glad. He seems a kind and caring boy." Angela's eyes ran over the rainbow array of cupcakes. She chose a cup cake with pink icing, topped with a dark pink flower topped with small silver balls.

"I'll have a chocolate cup cake."

"Jacob's been telling me his plans of becoming a pilot."

"*Jah*, I've heard those plans too. I used to have fancy plans when I was his age, before I knew better."

"Robert, I didn't know that Jacob was adopted."

Robert put his head to the side. "He told you?"

Angela nodded. "Not that's it's any of my business, but from what he's said, his biological *daed* died and now both his adoptive parents have died. Must be hard on him."

Robert nodded. "He doesn't have things so bad. He's got me and he's got a home here."

Of course, he'd have to think of the positive side of things, Angela thought. "He talks of his biological *daed's schweschder*. Does she live close by?"

Robert lowered his head and was silent for a moment. "I don't allow her around him."

Angela remained silent, waiting for him to continue.

"It disturbs me to speak of her or even think of Jacob's *daed's schweschder*, Juliana Redcliffe. She was the one who was the witness against Ross. It seems as though because Ross told her to stay away from Jacob that she was out to get him in whatever way she could."

"Juliana Redcliffe was the one who said she saw Ross hit the man on the head, Jacob's *ant*?"

Robert nodded.

"How do you know this?" Angela asked.

"Ross told me about her. It was common knowledge at the time; everyone knew. Made it all up, of course. Seems she wanted to get back at Ross for some reason."

"Why?"

"She wanted to visit Jacob, and Ross wouldn't have it. Ross wanted Jacob to be brought up Amish and not have the influence of the outside world. That woman would have brought the outside world into his life. She already filled his head with pilot nonsense."

"He spoke to me of her, so he must have met her at some point," Angela said.

"*Jah,* he did meet her. She went against my *bruder's* wishes and spoke to him several times when he walked home from *skul.* It went on for a while before someone told Ross that they saw an *Englisch* woman speaking to Jacob. Ross knew who it would be straight away."

Angela broke off a piece of cupcake and popped it in her mouth.

"That woman filled Jacob's head with nonsense of his *daed* being a pilot."

"Was he a pilot?" Angela asked.

"I'm not sure what he was. Ross would have known. All I knew is that Ross' *fraa,* Linda, met Jacob's biological *mudder* somewhere. She wasn't interested in bringing up the child. She wanted to adopt him out and that's all I know of his birth parents. That's all I was told."

"Do you have any idea of the name of the man who died? Any idea at all?"

Robert shook his head from side to side and looked across at her. "What have you heard?"

"I've heard that the man was Juliana Redcliffe's boyfriend or live-in lover or such. I guess that could be just a rumor and no one seems to know his name." Angela knew she wasn't supposed to tell Robert anything until the widows found out more, but now that he knew a lot more than he'd been admitting to, she considered that it no longer mattered.

"*Jah*, I heard the same," Robert said.

"Robert, this gives Juliana a motive. A motive to have your *bruder* blamed for something. It's a vital piece of information."

Robert rubbed his forehead hard.

"Do you think that she deliberately blamed Ross?" Angela asked.

"I'm sure of it. I didn't want to tell you about it before. I wanted to see what you'd find out, or rather what Elsa-May might find out, without any influence from me."

Angela blew out a deep breath. "I understand that, but the police don't know that Juliana, the witness against Ross, was Jacob's biological *ant* or that she knew the murdered man. Don't you think that you should tell them, and also tell them that she was trying to talk to Jacob and Ross told her to stay away? The detective said to Emma that there was nothing linking the witness to Ross. Ross must have never told the police."

Robert rubbed his ear. "Ross would have been confident that the truth would come out eventually."

"*Nee*, that doesn't seem right. It would have got Ross off straight away, I'm sure of it. It's a major fact and I don't know why you haven't made a point of telling the police. There must be more to it."

"Every time I'd find out a piece of information I'd go in and tell the police. I kept going in there to tell them different things I found out, but they got irritable with me and didn't want to know. I don't know what more I can do. I even wrote them a letter explaining everything to them."

Angela knew it couldn't have been easy for Robert to speak of such delicate things to someone he'd only just met. Maybe she should talk of something else, but she could not get the whole murder incident off her mind. "Tell me if I am missing something. No one knows the identity of the murdered *mann*? The witness who named Ross as the murderer was Jacob's biological *ant*?"

"That's what I'm sure of."

Angela wound the string of her prayer *kapp* around her finger. "Have you thought that the dead man might be Jacob's biological father?"

Robert's face remained expressionless and he slowly said, "I have considered it, but it would be too terrible a thing."

Angela said, "The police said that they have a DNA sample, so all they would need is a swab from Jacob to see if they are a match. That way you'd know for certain."

Robert shook his head. "He already knows both his *daeds* died so how would that help him?"

"It's a piece in the puzzle to find who the real killer was, so your *bruder's* name will clear."

Robert cleared his throat. "Either way, it's upsetting for him."

"You're right. It's upsetting either way. You have to decide what's more important to you and what's more important to Jacob. Surely it's *gut* to know the truth on a matter."

"It's a bad situation. It seems as whatever way I turn or

whatever I tell the police, no *gut* will come of anything." Robert's eyes went glassy as if he was close to tears.

Angela put her hand comfortingly on his shoulder.

"It's been nice talking to you. I've had this burden on my own for so long that it's a relief to speak about it with someone. *Denke* for taking such an interest in us," Robert said.

CHAPTER 9

But as many as received Him, to them He gave the right to become children of God, to those who believe in His name
John 1:12

WHEN ANGELA PULLED the buggy up outside Emma's *haus*, Emma came out to meet her.

"I'll tend to the horse," Emma said.

"I've got a lot to tell you, Emma." Angela got out of the buggy.

"Follow me and and tell me," Emma said while she led the horse into the stable.

"The witness, Juliana Redcliffe, was Jacob's biological *ant*, and Robert's also heard the rumor that the dead man was living with Juliana."

Emma stopped walking the horse for a moment and

looked at her. "Angela that is a huge piece of information. That would have set Ross free if that connection between the two of them was known."

"Robert said that Ross told him that the birth *mudder* did not want to have anything to do with the child and they had no more contact with her. Juliana was visiting the boy and telling him about his real *daed* on the way home from *skul* and when Ross found out, he told her to stay away. I got to wondering whether the dead man might be Jacob's birth father."

"I never even considered that. *Gut* work finding all that out. We should go visit Elsa-May tomorrow and tell her everything. Had Robert know all this for a while?"

"*Jah*, he did, but he kept it from me. He said he wanted to see what Elsa-May would uncover."

"Be *gut* if he could've told you everything from the start. Would've saved a lot of time," Emma said.

"Don't you think it would've been hard for him to tell a total stranger everything? It was awkward at first when I tried to explain who I was and he knew nothing about the letters." Angela giggled. "He must have thought I was quite mad until he figured out that Jacob wrote the letters."

"I guess so. He seems to like you."

"You think he does?"

"I'm sure he does. He'd be doing well to have a fine woman like you as his *fraa*. He would well know it too."

The next morning after breakfast Emma said to Angela, "I'll quickly go to Wil's *haus* to use his phone and have the widows meet together this afternoon."

Emma wrapped her black shawl around her shoulders and walked the five minutes to Wil's *haus*.

"Emma, I didn't expect to see you this morning." Wil stuck his head around the barn door when he saw Emma approach the *haus*.

"Hello, Wil. I've just come by to borrow your phone if I may. I just need to phone Elsa-May for a minute."

"Sure, come in."

The phone was in the barn on the back wall. Emma was sure to keep her voice low so Wil would not ask her questions when she got off the phone.

"Elsa-May, can you organize for the widows to all meet this afternoon? I have news of the witness's identity and we have a theory on who the dead man might be."

"Who was he?"

"Robert seems to think that it just might be Jacob's biological father; although he has no idea of the man's name. According to Angela, Robert knows that the witness is Jacob's biological *ant*. She even told Jacob that she's his real *daed's schweschder*. The police don't even know the connection."

Elsa-May was silent for a time.

"Are you still there, Elsa-May?" Emma asked.

"*Jah*, I'm still here. I'm trying to work things out. Did she think that she saw Jacob's *daed* kill him or did she make the whole thing up, or did she see someone else kill him?"

Emma said, "Maybe she wasn't at the scene of the crime at all and didn't see anyone. She could have just made the whole thing up."

"What reason would she have to make it up? Did she have something against Ross?" Elsa-May asked.

"Robert told Angela that the *schweschder* was talking to Jacob for a time every afternoon as he walked home from *skul*. Ross found out and warned her to stay away. He didn't want anyone from the outside world talking to his boy."

"Okay, that might have made her annoyed with him," Elsa-May said.

"*Jah,* but annoyed enough to have him charged for murder?" Emma glanced up to see if Wil looked like he was listening.

"That's what we'll have to find out. I'll have Crowley come to the meeting as well. He'll need to know what we've found out," Elsa-May said.

"*Jah,* okay." Emma looked up to see Wil looking over at her. She remembered she told Wil she'd only be quick. "I'll see you this afternoon, Elsa-May." Emma hung up the phone.

"Everything all right, Emma?"

Emma walked toward Wil. "*Jah,* everything is fine."

"You know, you can tell me things. If there's any kind of trouble, I'd like to know about it."

Emma shook her head. "I know you would and if there was any trouble, or if I was in any kind of trouble, you would be the first to know."

Wil smiled revealing his straight white teeth. "You had breakfast yet?"

"*Jah,* I have. I'd better get back to Angela. I told her I'd only be a little while."

"I never see much of you when you have visitors." Wil

walked toward her and put his strong arm around her back.

Emma giggled. "I hardly ever have visitors."

"*Kumm*, I'll walk you back home." They held hands until they got out of the barn and then Emma broke her hand gently from his grip. She did not feel it proper to have too much physical contact until they were married; even though she craved his touch, she knew that she would have to wait.

They took the usual short cut through the fields.

"I've been giving some thought to where we should live." Wil looked down at his feet as he walked.

"*Jah*? What have you thought about?"

"We could build a *haus* between the two properties. Half on your side and half on my side. Come here." He took hold of Emma's hand and they walked up a little rise. "Right here. What about that?"

Emma looked around about her. The land was slightly higher than the surrounding land and there were *gut* views of both properties. "It seems like a nice place for a *haus*."

"We could have the porch right here." Wil raised his arm across in front of him. "We could sit here of a morning drinking *kaffe* and look at all this."

Emma looked to where he was waving his arms to see the soft yellow wheat blowing in the wind. Clumps of dark green trees in the distance framed the wheat fields. "It's certainly a pretty site, but is it practical, Wil? We'd have to build another barn, as well as a chicken coup and a …"

Wil laughed. "Listen to you. If I can build you a *haus*, I

can certainly build a barn, a chicken coup and whatever else we need. I'll rent my *haus* out and you can do what you like with your *haus*. Leave it vacant, let friends stay, whatever you wish."

Emma turned her eyes back to the swaying fronds of wheat and tried to imagine what it would be like to sip *kaffe* there in the mornings in their own new *haus*. "*Ach*, Wil. I'd love it. I'd love it."

"*Gut*, I'll get working on the plans right away."

Emma smiled and tried to still her mind as it tried to wander back to the time when Levi was drawing up plans for their *haus*. *Levi's in the past*, she reminded herself as she consciously blocked out the memories. She knew she had to enjoy the present moments with Wil and not have memories of the past ruin what happiness she could have right now.

Wil put his arm around her waist. "We'll be happy here, Emma."

She pressed into his arms and tipped her head up to look into his kind eyes. "I know, I just know we will."

They held each other tightly for a moment before Emma pulled away. "Angela will be wondering what's taking me so long."

As they continued on their way to Emma's *haus*, Wil said, "You never told me whether Angela and Robert liked each other."

Emma laughed. "That's quite a story. It seems that Jacob was writing the letters to Angela."

"Little Jacob?"

"*Jah*, he was writing to her pretending to be Robert."

Wil shook his head. "That's an embarrassment for both Angela and Robert."

"I suppose so, but it seems they like each other now they've met. Angela went back to visit him yesterday. Things look *gut* for the two of them."

"Must be difficult for Robert to look after the boy by himself. He seems to be spirited from what I've heard. I know it can't be easy for the boy losing both his parents in that accident."

Once they had arrived at Emma's *haus*, Emma said, "You coming in for a *kaffe*, Wil?"

Wil looked up at the h*aus*. "*Nee*, I've got plans to start on."

Emma looked into his eyes and smiled. "I'll see you soon then."

Wil kissed Emma lightly on her forehead then turned back toward his *haus*.

CHAPTER 10

But thou, when thou prayest, enter into thy closet, and when thou hast shut thy door, pray to thy Father which is in secret; and thy Father which seeth in secret shall reward thee openly.
Matthew 6:6

THAT AFTERNOON the widows all gathered at Elsa-May and Ettie's *haus.* Angela told the ladies all they found out before Detective Crowley arrived.

"Thank you for coming, Detective," Elsa-May said.

"It sounded important." The detective sat on a creaky, wooden chair opposite the widows. "What can I do for you ladies?" Detective Crowley looked straight at Emma and gave her a glowing smile. Emma looked away because he had a way of making her feel uneasy, as if she had committed some type of crime.

Elsa-May told Crowley all about the suspected identity of the dead man and the identity of the witness.

"When it was mentioned to have Jacob do a DNA test, Robert wasn't agreeable," Emma said.

The detective was silent for a while. "The boy would've been through enough. I can understand Robert not wanting to put the boy through any more dramas." The detective scratched his chin and after a moment said, "What we can do is match the boy's birth certificate records to find his biological father's name. Once we have his name, we'll try and find his dental records and match them up to the records from the dead man's autopsy."

"*Jah*, brilliant idea," Elsa-May said.

Detective Crowley smiled at Elsa-May, "I'll get straight on to that today."

Silvie said, "If it is proven that the witness did have some kind of relationship to the dead man then would that be enough to clear Ross's name? Especially since the woman was keeping information from the police?"

"Possibly; it's not up to me. It seems there's much more to this whole case than what it first appeared. Why don't we meet back here the same time tomorrow?" Crowley said. "That should give me enough time to find Jacob's birth father's name."

THE NEXT DAY, Angela and the other ladies kept the appointment with Detective Crowley at Elsa-May and Ettie's *haus*.

"I found the name of Jacob's biological father from his

birth certificate. His name is Wesley Conrad and he's still alive and well, living in California. We contacted him this morning. He claims he ceased all contact with his sister some years ago, and last he heard of her she was living in England. What's more, her description does not fit the description of the witness."

Crowley pulled a notebook from his pocket and read his notes. "Wesley Conrad is not a pilot and he works for civil service. He has no wish for any contact with the boy that he gave up for adoption. He said that he barely knew the mother of the baby. He continued to say that he suggested to the mother that she abort the baby and she refused. She eventually agreed to adopt. Wesley heard that after she gave the baby up, she tried to get him back."

"Who is the mother; did you find that out detective?" Emma asked.

"Ah, that's the bit I was saving 'til last. The mother's name is Juliana Redcliffe."

The widows gasped.

"That's right. Jacob's birth mother, the woman who is named on his birth certificate, is the woman who has claimed to witness Ross killing the man."

Angela asked, "Why would she tell Jacob that she was his *ant*, when she's really his *mudder*?"

"Most likely she didn't want the boy to get confused by having two mothers, who knows," the detective said.

Ettie said, "If the witness is the mother, why would she wish harm on Ross?"

Angela said, "Robert said that Ross warned her to keep away from Jacob. He would've known who she was."

Elsa-May said, "Have you talked to Juliana again now that you've got the new information, Detective?"

"Not yet. I'm going to see her tomorrow in the afternoon. Just wanted to check with you ladies first, to see if you've found out anything else." Detective Crowley leaned forward, stretched out his hand and took a chocolate slice. "Mmm, this is very nice."

Maureen said, "Emma made those."

Emma glared at Maureen wishing she had not said that. The detective smiled at Emma and Emma managed to force a smile back at him.

"As I was saying, I'll go and see the woman and see what she says about the whole thing." The detective continued to bite into the slice.

Ettie said, "Why didn't all this information come out before? Why wasn't more investigation done into it?"

The detective swallowed his mouthful. "With no known identity of the deceased and with the arrested man dead, the case came to a stand still. We still don't know the murdered man's identity."

"Convenient wasn't it? The investigation ceased because Ross died; might not one suppose that Ross was killed to prevent further investigations?" Elsa-May said.

Ettie pushed a bony finger into the air. "Yes, the real killer might have killed Ross off to cover his tracks."

"Or hers," Silvie said.

The detective licked chocolate from his lips. "I've already thought of that. I checked into the buggy accident that killed Mr. and Mrs. Geiger and there were no suspicious circumstances. None whatsoever."

"Can you double check, detective?" Elsa-May asked.

"No point. I checked it all again this morning. It was a drunk driver who was already known to the police. He was badly injured and was charged with manslaughter. There's no connection to him whatsoever." The detective brushed some crumbs from around his lips and stood up. "I'll check back in with you ladies after I speak to Juliana Redcliffe tomorrow."

Ettie pushed her lips tightly together. Emma knew that Ettie was not convinced that there was no connection, particularly when no one knew the connection of the witness and the dead man until very recently.

When the detective left Ettie said to Silvie, "Onto a happier subject. Elsa-May and I have a surprise for you, Silvie."

"For me?" Silvie smiled brightly. "What is it?"

"Bailey is coming to stay nearby for two days next week. He called us today to let us know. Since you have no phone he would've arrived before a letter reached you."

Silvie clasped her hands together. "He is? He's coming?"

"*Jah*, and I'd say he's only coming to see you. He said to be sure and tell you. He was going to keep it as a surprise, but he only has two days here and he didn't want you to be off doing something else when he got here."

Silvie's face beamed for the remainder of the evening.

"Who's Bailey?" Angela asked.

"Bailey is Ettie and Elsa-May's nephew; he's a detective," Emma said.

"*Ach, jah*, I've heard about him from Elsa-May," Angela said.

"He's not a relative of yours too, Angela?" Maureen asked.

"*Nee*, I'm related to Elsa-May's late husband."

Emma continued to explain who Bailey was. "Bailey stayed with Wil months ago when he was working undercover. He was pretending he wanted to become Amish and he fell in love with Silvie."

"That's romantic," Angela said.

"Well, it wasn't too romantic when I found out that he wasn't who he said he was," Silvie said. "I know it was his job and everything, but it was still deceiving people."

Emma said, "He was sorry about it. He didn't intend to hurt anyone. Now, he might even come and join the community."

"Really?" Elsa-May and Ettie chimed together.

"He said that again, just recently?" Elsa-May asked.

Angela frowned at Emma. "Emma. That was something private I told you."

Emma's hand flew to her mouth. "I'm sorry, Silvie. I forgot. I was just excited about it."

Silvie looked at both Ettie and Elsa-May. "I didn't want to tell anyone his thoughts unless they didn't happen."

"That would be *wunderbaar* if he joined the community," Ettie said. "It would be a real answer to prayer."

"We'll have to wait and see. No *gut* getting excited about something that might not ever happen," Elsa-May said.

"But it might happen, Elsa-May. Why can't you ever let me be happy about anything?" Ettie asked.

The other ladies looked at each other and smiled; they

were used to Elsa-May and Ettie getting under each other's skin.

"You can be happy about whatever you want, Ettie. I'm just saying that he might not join us. Why get excited about something that might never happen? It doesn't make sense. He only said that he might, and he only told Silvie in private. He likely doesn't want anyone to know his private thoughts, only Silvie."

Ettie lowered her head. "I won't say anything to anyone, Silvie."

Emma said, "*Nee*, we'll all keep quiet about it. Sorry for mentioning it, Silvie; I was just happy for you."

"No harm done," Silvie said.

Elsa-May turned her attention to Angela. "Angela, I had a call from Robert just before everyone arrived just now. He wanted to know if he could call on you tomorrow morning at Emma's *haus*."

Angela gasped and drew both hands to her mouth. "What did you say?"

"I said *jah,* of course."

Maureen said, "Angela, you seem to like Robert quite a bit."

"I do like him, but he just probably wants to know what I've found out so far."

"*Nee*, he asked me questions. He wants to see you, plain and simple," Elsa-May said. Elsa-May and Ettie had a telephone in a shanty outside their *haus*. Elsa-May also kept a cell-phone for emergencies that very few people knew about as it would be very much frowned upon to have such a modern convenience.

Angela's face glowed just as Silvie's glowed.

"I'm feeling all left out now," Maureen said. "Everyone's got *menner* but me." She looked at Elsa-May and Ettie. "Do you have *gut* news for me? Has any *mann* called you for me?"

Everyone laughed except Elsa-May, who looked quite serious. "Ettie and I don't have anyone," she said.

"You two don't want anyone, do you?" Emma asked.

Ettie chuckled, "I'm too old now. I might have been interested years ago."

"I'm too old and set in my ways now," Elsa-May said.

Silvie asked, "What happened with Bob Pluver, Maureen?"

Emma shivered at Bob Pluver's name. She found him an odd character.

"I went to dinner with him a few months ago." Maureen's mouth turned down at the sides. "He hardly said a word."

"He never says much, Maureen. You never know what's going on in his head. That's what unnerves me about the man." Emma bit her lip. She often spoke without thinking and this was one of those times. "I'm sorry; I didn't mean to be unkind."

"It's hard to get to know someone if they don't speak," Maureen said.

"Do you like him?" Ettie asked Maureen.

Maureen gave a little shrug of her shoulders. "I think I do, a little."

"He might need a little encouragement. I heard his *daed* was hard on him and used to beat him. *Spare the rod and spoil the child* was his saying. I heard he didn't spare the rod at all. That has to have affected him and made him unsure of himself," Elsa-May said.

"I need a *mann* who'll look after me. I don't want to be a *mudder* to a *mann*," Maureen said.

"I agree with you," Emma said.

"He might have potential in the future," Maureen said.

"If he changes?" Emma asked.

"*Jah*," Maureen agreed.

Silvie put her arm around Maureen's shoulder. "You never know who *Gott's* got for you."

"His ways are not our ways," Ettie said with a smile.

Maureen smiled and nodded.

ROBERT SAID he'd be there at 10 a.m. the very next day. Angela had been ready and waiting since 9 a.m. She was excited to spend time with Robert. Jacob would be in *skul* so they would have no distractions. Angela wondered where they would go.

"Excited I see?" Emma said.

"*Jah*. It's been a while since I've had the interest of a man. My heart keeps beating fast." Angela put her hand lightly over her heart.

"I suppose you don't know where he's taking you?"

"Elsa-May didn't say. Maybe he's taking me back to his *haus* to talk some more."

"I'm glad you've come to stay with me. It's been nice having someone else around. Someone else in the *haus* besides Growler."

"I've never lived alone, always with *mamm* and *daed*.

I've got three cats at home. I've an old white fluffy one, a ginger tabby kitten and a black cat. The white one is the only one allowed in the *haus*. The other two are happy to prowl around and catch mice."

"I never liked cats until I got Growler. He's not friendly, but he's *gut* company for me."

Angela laughed. "Cats can be moody sometimes."

Emma nodded her head. "*Ach*, sounds like that might be Robert."

Angela dashed to the window. "*Jah*, it is." Angela smoothed down the apron that covered most of her dress and touched her prayer *kapp* to be sure it sat properly on her head. "See you later today, Emma."

"Goodbye." Emma stayed inside the *haus* and watched them drive away. The look on Robert's face as Angela walked toward the buggy confirmed Emma's suspicions that Robert liked Angela very much.

Emma hurried to Elsa-May *haus* as early that same morning Wil had delivered a message that Emma was to go to Elsa-May's *haus* as soon as Angela left. Emma knew that meant that an urgent widows' meeting had been called.

CHAPTER 11

And whatever things you ask in prayer,
believing, you will receive
Matthew 21:22

As soon as they were clear of Emma's *haus*, Angela glanced at Robert's face and he caught her eye and smiled.

"I read all your letters last night," Robert said.

Angela's face lighted up. "You did? I didn't realize that Jacob would've kept them all."

"He did, and he presented them to me last night."

Angela lowered her head and looked at the floor of the buggy. "*Ach*, now I'm embarrassed."

"No need to be embarrassed, you wrote from your heart with honesty. That's commendable."

Angela put her fingertips to her eyes. "I wish you hadn't read them."

"They were addressed to me and they were my letters." He turned to her and said softly, "I'm glad I read them. I know you much better now."

"Not fair. You know me better now than I know you. You should write me forty letters to catch up."

Robert chuckled. "While you're here, I would like to get to know you better and have you get to know me."

Angela swallowed hard which turned into almost a gulp; she hoped he hadn't heard it over the clip clop of the horse's hooves. "I'd like that."

He looked over at her and smiled. The warmth of his face sent pulses through her body like she'd never known before.

"Jacob must have written to you in a mature manner for you to think a grown man penned the letters."

"I can show you my letters. I've got them at Emma's place. He wrote well. I had no idea, no idea at all. He spoke of mature things. Jacob has a *gut* insight on life. He must care for you deeply to be hunting for a *fraa* for you."

"Angela, I'm glad that he wrote to you and had you come to visit. I know what he did was wrong, but I would never have written back to someone. If I got that first letter from you I most likely would have written back telling you that I was too busy to write or some such thing. It worked out well that Jacob replied to you."

Angela remained silent because she did not know how to respond to his candid admission of interest in her. Should she appear keen? She had already shown how keen she was to get married by writing to a *mann* whom she did not know. If she said that she was interested in him too, that might appear as if she were desperate to marry a *mann* – any *mann.*

Robert took his eyes off the road and glanced at Angela again. "Forgive me, I always say what's on my mind. I think that's always the best way. You are a lovely woman."

A giggle escaped Angela's lips, which released the tension she felt just seconds before.

"Any *mann* would be pleased to have you as his *fraa.*"

Angela searched her mind for a reply. Any reply would be better than remaining silent yet, she was not accustomed to speaking to *menner,* especially not ones as handsome as Robert.

"In your letters you mentioned that you were looking to marry," Robert said.

Angela nodded knowing that she could admit to wanting marriage as all the girls in the community wanted a happy *familye.* "I am. I'm looking for a *gut mann* to marry and raise a *familye* with. What about you?" Angela silently reprimanded herself for her blunt question. She might have been better off to remain silent after all.

"I'd like nothing more to have a *fraa* and *kinner,* but I need to get Jacob settled first. I've taken on Jacob as my responsibility. I'd like to clear his *daed's* name and then I would feel free to live my life and find a *fraa.*"

"I understand. Jacob's very blessed to have someone who cares for him so deeply." They sat next to each other in silence as the buggy clip clopped through the winding, narrow roads. Angela was at peace in Robert's company. There was something about being with Robert that made her feel safe. As well as his obvious physical strength, she sensed that he also had an inner strength.

"I'm taking you to my favorite place," Robert said.

"Where's that?"

Robert laughed. "There's an old stone bridge not far up here. I used to play underneath the bridge when I was a child. I would fish from the top of it as well. I haven't been there in a long time."

"I'd love to see it."

Robert pulled the buggy off the road and tied the horse in the shade. "It's just down here."

Robert held Angela's hand and helped her through the undergrowth. They walked a little further until the bridge came into view.

"Is that it, Robert? It's beautiful."

"That's it all right." As soon as they were on the bridge, Robert said, "It's called a kissing bridge." He glanced at Angela. "Don't look worried. That's what they're called, but I didn't know that until recently."

"Why's it called a kissing bridge?"

Robert looked over the edge of the bridge. "They're romantic places to go, I'd guess."

Angela looked at the reflective surface of the water as it rippled its way underneath the bridge. The birds chirping and the rustle of the wind in the treetops made a perfect melody for their special time alone.

It's a perfect place for a first kiss, Angela thought. *I wonder if that's why he brought me here.* She looked up at Robert. He took his eyes off the horizon and looked deeply into her eyes. He moved his body so it was directly in front of hers. He caressed the side of her face with his fingertips. Her body shuddered at his touch, however she did not move away.

"Your skin is so smooth." Robert's words were whispered.

She smiled at his compliment, but words escaped her. All she could think on was what his mouth would feel like against hers. Angela had never desired to be kissed by a man until that very moment.

As if he sensed her longing, his gaze fell to her mouth. He lowered his head until his lips lingered over hers. Was he asking for her permission to touch her lips? She arched her back and moved her lips just a fraction until their lips met.

All feeling left Angela's body and her head began to swim. She was not aware that blackness had engulfed her until she woke with her body on the hard ground and her head cradled in Robert's manly arms. She made to move.

"*Nee*, stay still. You've fainted; it must be the heat."

Angela obeyed his command, closed her eyes and enjoyed being close to him, inhaling his manly aroma.

Angela was aware that it was a hot day, but was that why she fainted? Surely it was the closeness of Robert's hard, body and his soft lips against hers that caused her to loose consciousness. "I'm alright."

He lifted her head up a little.

"I don't know what happened," Angela said.

"Have you been unwell?"

"*Nee*, I'm always in *gut* health."

"It's a hot day. Stay here. I've got some water in the buggy." Robert helped position Angela's back against the side of the bridge.

While Robert fetched the water, Angela recalled that she had not drank any water the entire day, when normally she drank quite a few glasses by this time of the day. Angela admired how caring and attentive Robert was. She touched her lips softly with her fingertips as she remembered their kiss.

"Here you go." He poured the water from a large container into a metal cup.

She slowly drank two cups of water. "I remembered that I hadn't drank any water at all today."

Robert sat down next to her. "I said that it was a kissing bridge, not a fainting bridge."

Angela smiled. "Did I dream that we kissed?"

Robert whispered. "That was real."

His whispers sent tingles soaring down her back. They sat and talked for a time and they didn't even notice that dark rain clouds had gathered overhead. Raindrops began to spatter down upon them in large droplets. They both looked upwards at the gray sky.

"We're going to get caught in the rain," Robert said.

"Moments ago it was bright sunshine."

They looked at each other and laughed.

Never had Angela dreamed it would be possible to have such a time with a man. She knew now what she had missed out on. Being quiet and shy had done her no favors in the past. But if she hadn't kept away from *menner* she might be married to someone else by now and she would never have gotten to meet Robert.

"Are you all right to stand?" Robert asked.

"I'm sure I am."

Robert put his arm around her waist and pulled her to her feet. "Let's go."

Once they were both inside the buggy the rain began to pour down in shafts.

"I made a picnic for us. I imagined we would sit in the sun on a grassy bank overlooking my bridge. How would you feel about eating here in the buggy?"

"*Jah*, let's have the picnic right here in the buggy."

Robert reached over to the backseat and unwrapped a package of ham and relish buns. "The weather's not usually like this here. It usually stays as it starts out in the morning. We don't normally get sudden downfalls of rain like this."

"I love the rain, especially at night. I love to hear it beating against the window pain and pouring down the pipes at the side of the *haus*," Angela said.

CHAPTER 12

Surely goodness and mercy shall follow me all the days of my
life: and I will dwell in the house of the Lord for ever.
Psalms 23:6

WHILE ANGELA WAS WITH ROBERT, Emma was at the emergency widows' meeting that had been called. Detective Crowley was to meet them again that afternoon.

"I heard that Juliana took a different man home with her nearly every weekend. The particular weekend when that man was murdered, she had left the bar with the same man for the third Saturday in a row. It was a Saturday, wasn't it, that the murder took place?" The widows all nodded so Ettie continued, "Why would she go for a walk on her own because she couldn't sleep? What's more, she was seen leaving with the man by more than one staff member of the bar."

"Why hasn't this come out before? Why don't the police know about it?" Silvie asked.

"She told the police that she was alone, but she wasn't. The police wouldn't have known to ask the bar staff because they wouldn't have known she was there in the first place," Ettie said.

"You think that the man murdered was the same man taken home by Juliana that night?" Emma asked.

Ettie nodded. "He fits the description and no one knew him; he wasn't from around here, from what the bar staff told me."

Silvie said, "How do they remember something from so long ago?"

Ettie said, "Marg, one of the staff, was concerned when she heard of the murder. She even asked Juliana about it. Marg asked Juliana if she'd seen the man alive after that time. Juliana told her that the man she'd taken home couldn't have been the same man who was murdered because he was at her house when she'd gone for that walk. The walk where she said she saw Ross hit that man over the head."

Ettie took a deep breath and continued. "Marg asked Juliana why the man wasn't around any longer and Juliana said she'd sent him on his way because he'd gotten violent with her. She even showed Marg bruises on her arm, two days after the murder."

"Did Marg ever think to go to the police? Or were the police aware that Juliana had someone staying at her *haus* the night of the murder?"

"The detective didn't mention a thing about it." Ettie turned to Elsa-May. "Did he mention anything to you?"

"*Nee* he didn't. I've spoken to him twice about that murder and he never once mentioned that she had some strange man at her house that night," Elsa-May said. "Silvie, why don't you knock on Juliana's door and pretend you're from the college doing a paper on witnesses and ask her if she wouldn't mind answering some questions?"

Silvie's face went pale. "Why me? I can't do things like that. I wouldn't know what to ask. I can't fool someone like that. She'd never believe me. Amish don't go to college, so how do I explain that?"

"*Jah* she will believe you, I'll write the questions for you and you'll have to get yourself some clothes that will pass as *Englisch*. All you say when she answers the door is, *Good morning. Are you Juliana Redcliffe? I'm Silvie Brown and I'm doing a paper on the effect that witnessing a crime has on people. Do you mind if I ask you some questions?* She'll either say *no* and slam the door on you or invite you in. If she invites you in, you'll produce my list of questions and write down her answers. It's simple, Silvie," Elsa-May said.

Silvie nodded, "*Jah*, I suppose I can do that, but I'm a little frightened. What if she killed that man and blamed it on Ross? That means I'll be alone with a murderer."

Elsa-May tapped her chin. "I'll have Maureen go with you."

Maureen pulled a sour face. "All right, I'll go with you, Silvie. As long as you do all the talking; you're better at that kind of thing than me."

"You need to do that today. There's no time to waste. You have to speak to Juliana and make sure you don't bump into Crowley; he wouldn't be too happy to see you anywhere near Juliana," Elsa-May said.

~

AN HOUR LATER, Silvie and Maureen, both wearing *Englisch* clothes, pulled up in a taxi up the road from Juliana's house.

When the taxi drove away, Silvie said, "I hope she's home. Remember, I'll do all the talking and you help me take notes on what she says."

Half an hour before, when they were at Silvie's *haus* dressing in *Englisch* clothes, it occurred to Silvie and Maureen to go against Elsa-May's advice. They hoped they would not get into terrible trouble with her. They decided rather than say that they were doing a paper on witnessing crime they would say that they were doing a survey for the Department of Health on violence against women. Maybe that would have her open up about the man who was violent with her.

They had the taxi drop them a little up the road so it would appear as though they were doing a door-to-door survey.

They knocked on Juliana's door, hoping that she would be home.

Seconds later a woman who answered Juliana's description answered the door.

Maureen spoke first. "Hello, we're doing a survey."

"We're from the health department," Silvie added.

The woman looked from one to the other. "What's it about?"

"It's about violence against women. We're trying to find how wide spread it actually is and we're going door to door in the whole neighborhood," Silvie said, hoping that *Gott* would forgive her for telling a fib if it was to help someone.

"Do you have five minutes to answer some quick questions?" Maureen asked.

Juliana looked at her watch. "As long as it will only be five minutes."

"That's all it will take," Maureen said.

"Come in then." Juliana stepped back so both women could enter the *haus*. "This way." She took them through to a small room with two small couches. "Have a seat."

Once they were seated, Silvie shuffled some papers in readiness to make it look as though she was reading questions out.

"I forgot to ask for your ID," Juliana said.

"We don't have any yet," Maureen said.

"There was a mix-up with the new model of ID and they'll be ready tomorrow. We can call back and show you tomorrow if you wish," Silvie said.

Juliana shook her head, "Don't worry about it. Will this survey help other women?"

"That's the purpose of it," Silvie said. Without written questions from Elsa-May and with no time to write any of her own, Silvie had to pull some quick questions from her head. "Have you ever been the victim of abuse?"

"Yes, I have. I've been physically abused many times in my life."

Maureen leaned forward. "Have you? That's awful."

After an intense stare from Silvie, Maureen straightened up.

"Thank you and yes, it was awful. First my step-father beat me on more than one occasion and I had two boyfriends who used to hit me when they got angry."

Juliana cast her tear filled eyes downward and Silvie looked at Maureen. Had they bitten off more than they could chew?

"When was the last time you experienced abuse? Could you tell us about it? If you feel you can talk about it," Maureen said.

Juliana sniffed and looked at the two ladies in front of her. "It was a while ago now. I made sure that he could never hurt anyone again."

"That's good and how did you see to that?" Silvie asked.

Juliana shook her head. "I don't want to speak about it. In fact, I'd prefer not to talk at all. It's too upsetting for me to speak about." Juliana looked at Silvie and then looked at Maureen. "I appreciate what you ladies are doing. There's too much violence towards women. I hope you can make a change, but I can't help you." Juliana rose to her feet. "I'll show you out."

Maureen stayed seated. "Before we leave can you tell me just how does one go about making sure that a man will never hit a woman again?"

Juliana shrugged her shoulders. "How should I know?"

Maureen locked eyes with Juliana. "You just said that you made sure that the last man who hurt you would never hurt anyone again."

"I've had enough questions for today. I'm done." Juliana stared at Maureen until she stood up.

"Okay, thank you," Maureen said.

Maureen and Silvie left Juliana's house and hurried to the main road. Maureen reached into the pocket of her long black *Englisch* looking skirt and took out Elsa-May's borrowed cell phone to call a taxi.

Once the call was made, Silvie asked, "What do you think of all that?"

Maureen placed the cell carefully back in her pocket. "Did you hear what she said? She said she made sure the last man who hurt her would never hurt anyone again. Do you think she was referring to the man who was murdered two years ago?"

"Could have been."

∿

THAT AFTERNOON the five widows waited for the detective at Elsa-May and Ettie's *haus*. He had phoned ahead and told them that he had a significant development in the case of Ross Geiger.

"What news do you have for us, Detective?" Elsa-May asked once the detective sat on one of their hard, wooden chairs.

"Juliana Redcliffe admitted to killing the man and said that it was self-defense. She claimed that she witnessed Ross kill the man because she wanted him in jail so she could get her child back. She said that it was after she killed the man and was back in her house that she got the idea to make it look as though Ross had done it. She'd seen some sticks at the scene of the crime so she took some twine back to the body, made a cross and tied him to it. She figured it would be believable that an Amish man did it if there was a religious element there somewhere."

"But the dead man was found about 500 meters away from her house. How could she get him that far away?" Emma asked.

"He chased her out there. She claims he knocked her to the ground after chasing her from the house. She saw a rock and when he turned his head that's when she hit him. The first knock stunned him and he fell to the ground and she beat him with the rock a couple more times to make sure he would not get back up."

Emma winced as she imagined the scene.

"She kept the dead man's wallet, so now we know who he was and can try and contact his relatives." The detective yawned. "Excuse me."

"How did you get her to confess it all, after all this time?" Ettie asked.

"She thought we knew already. She said something about other people being there that morning to question her – two ladies." The detective looked at each lady in turn. He did not question any of them about the matter and neither did they comment.

"Will she go to jail?" Emma asked.

"Seems it was self defense so things would have gone better for her if she had admitted to it immediately. Now she's perverted the course of justice by her false accusation. The courts don't take things like that lightly."

"Do you think the buggy crash that killed Ross and Linda was purely an accident?" Ettie asked the detective.

"As I mentioned before, we found nothing suspicious to do with the buggy accident. It seemed to be just that – an accident," Detective Crowley said.

"I've got a *haus* guest so I better get going now. Thank you for helping us again, Detective." Emma said goodbye to everyone and hurried to her buggy. She was glad that Robert's *bruder*, Ross, would finally have his name cleared. Emma could hardly wait to go home and tell Angela the news.

Once Emma arrived back home, Angela was in her room and did not come out the whole night. It was the very next morning that Emma told Angela what the detective found out about Juliana and the murder.

"What should I do, Emma? Will I visit Robert, or should I wait for him to come here? What if he doesn't come here?" Angela asked over breakfast the next morning.

"Give it 'til after the midday meal and if he hasn't come here by then, take my buggy and go and visit him."

"*Denke*, Emma." Angela took a deep breath. "I hope the detective or someone lets him know what's going on."

"*Jah*, they would've told him. The detective knows how important it is for Robert to clear his *bruder's* name. That's what spurred this whole investigation. He has Robert's address and everything," Emma said.

CHAPTER 13

Let the word of Christ dwell in you richly in all wisdom;
teaching and admonishing one another in psalms and hymns
and spiritual songs, singing with grace in your hearts to
the Lord.
Colossians 3:16

BAILEY HAD ALREADY DELIVERED the bad news to Silvie through Elsa-May and Ettie. He could not stay two days at the nearby B&B as he had hoped, but he would drive to see her. They only could have a few small hours together before he would have to leave.

Silvie waited by the window for him. He told her that his car was dark gray in color and she fixed her eyes on the road looking for his car. A dark gray car turned off the road and into her driveway. She opened the door and waited for him in the doorway. Her heart pounded in her chest as she watched him walk toward her.

He walked quickly and reached out and held her tightly in his arms. "Oh, Silvie, I've missed you so much. So much."

"Me too." Silvie managed to say. He was holding her so tight she could barely speak. Silvie pulled him inside and shut the door.

"I need to say all that's on my mind. I've been giving things a lot of thought. In particular you and me, and joining the community," Bailey said.

Silvie raised her perfectly shaped eyebrows.

"I do want to come and join the community if the bishop will allow me. I'm hoping Wil will have me back to stay at his *haus*. He's easy to get on with and I'd feel awkward with a *familye* I didn't know. I might be ready in a year. How does that sound to you?"

"I would like it very much, but the bishop would tell you that you must join the community because that's what *Gott* has put on your heart to do, not because of us."

Bailey nodded. "I know he would say that, but without you I wouldn't be drawn here. Now that I've met you, I want to be with you forever."

Silvie was pleased by his words, but disappointed she would have to wait for him. "Why must you wait a whole year?"

"My job."

"Your job is still so important to you?"

"I feel a certain obligation toward the people who are depending on me. I'm so close to finding the stolen paintings I've been chasing."

Silvie raised her eyebrows again as she remembered him saying that he had been chasing those stolen paintings for a number of years.

"Will you wait for me, Silvie? I want to marry you, when I learn all the Amish ways and get baptized."

Silvie knew that she should have said *no* for two reasons. The first reason was that he was putting his job before *Gott* and herself, the second reason was that he should want to join the Amish whether she was there or not. Her head was conflicted with rights and wrongs, but her heart knew what it wanted. She heard herself say, "*Jah*, I'll wait for you, Bailey." The way she felt about him she had absolutely no choice.

"Thank you, Silvie. Thank you." Bailey took hold of her wrist and pulled her body to himself. As he held her tightly again he said, "You are more beautiful than I remember."

Their time together passed far too quickly for Silvie's liking. She watched with tears in her eyes as Bailey drove away from her.

"So, that's Bailey."

Silvie swung around to see her *schweschder*, Sabrina, walk out of the downstairs bedroom. "Sabrina, I didn't know that you were home."

"That sounded all very lovely dovey." Sabrina folded her arms as she walked towards Silvie.

Sabrina reminded Silvie of her *mudder*. That was exactly how her *mudder* would speak to her since she disapproved of everything Silvie did. "I love him, that's why," Silvie said, annoyed that Sabrina had overheard their private conversation.

"What would *mamm* think of you being in love with an *Englischer*? We're not supposed to be entangled with the world."

"Sabrina, you were obviously listening in on us so you would have heard him say that he's thinking of joining us."

Sabrina flung her arm in the air. "*Jah*, thinking not doing. There's a big difference. You even said yourself that his job was too important to him. Just because a handsome *Englischer* shows you a small bit of attention you go weak at the knees and put him before *Gott* and the community. You sounded all wimpy and childish when you were speaking to him. It made me sick to my stomach."

Silvie tipped her chin high. "I'm old enough to do what I wish and make my own decisions. I'm older than you, a lot older than you. Besides, you shouldn't have been listening to us."

Sabrina shook her head. "Older in years, but not in the head, it seems."

"You're staying here as my guest. I've a *gut* idea to pack you back off to *mamm* and *dat*," Silvie frowned and mirrored Sabrina by also crossing her arms firmly in front of her chest.

A look of horror crossed Sabrina's face. "You wouldn't do that, would you? I'm only trying to protect you from getting hurt by an *Englischer*."

"While you're under my roof, you will show me respect."

Sabrina pouted and stared at her *schweschder*. "All right, I won't say anymore about him."

"Are you sure? Not one word?" Silvie asked.

"I stayed away from Wil, didn't I, even though I had so much in common with him? I can keep to my word."

"I suppose that's true enough. You can stay then, but no telling *mamm* or anyone of any of my private information."

"All right, I won't. Can I stay?"

Silvie nodded and Sabrina turned around and hurried back into her room.

Silvie sank into the couch hoping she finally had Sabrina under control. Otherwise she surely would send her packing.

≈

ANGELA DID NOT HAVE to wait long for Robert to come to Emma's *haus.* The detective had visited him and told him all that had happened. Robert was shocked to find out that the woman who had spoken against his *bruder,* Ross, was Jacob's biological *mudder* and even more shocked that she admitted to killing the man and tying him to a cross so it would be more believable to blame an Amish man.

While Robert was at Emma's *haus,* he asked Angela to stay on in the community so they could see more of each other with a view to things becoming serious between them. Angela happily agreed. They drove away from Emma's *haus* to have a little time to themselves.

"You there, Emma?" Wil called out from Emma's front door.

Emma came to the door wiping her hands on a dishtowel. "Wil, come in."

"Robert and Angela just passed me in the buggy."

"*Jah*, they're getting along fine. Come into the kitchen; I'm baking cookies."

"Mmm, I thought I smelled something nice." Wil followed Emma to the kitchen and sat down. "I've been thinking about our *haus*."

"Our new one that you're doing the plans for?"

"Well, I don't know if that's the best way to go about things. With Bob leasing both of our farms, it's difficult to find the perfect spot for the *haus* that won't interfere with the land."

"Okay, so what have you been thinking?" Emma opened the oven door and peeked inside.

"I've got a couple of ideas. We could buy a house somewhere else, not too far from here, or we could buy land somewhere and build."

Emma pulled the cookie tray out of the oven. "I'll leave it up to you."

Wil leaped to his feet and took one of the hot cookies off the tray and tossed it in the air then from one hand to the other. "I'll start looking straight away." He leaned forward and gave Emma a quick kiss on the cheek then grabbed another cookie before he rushed out the door.

Emma giggled at how silly he was. He reminded her of a lively child who flitted from one project to another. She knew that when they were finally living together as *mann* and *fraa* that her life would never be dull or boring.

CHAPTER 14

*The blessing of him that was ready to perish came upon me: and
I caused the widow's heart to sing for joy.*
Job 29:13

A WEEK LATER, the five widows were gathered again at
Elsa-May and Ettie's *haus* for one of their regular widows'
meetings.

"Awful that Robert wanted to clear Jacob's *daed's* name
and then it turns out that Jacob's biological *mudder* was
the one who did the murder," Silvie said.

"*Nee*, it was self defense that's a very different thing to
murder," Maureen said.

"*Jah*, that's true," Silvie said.

"Angela tells me that Robert was very happy with the
outcome and he sent his thanks to all of us," Emma said.

"He's also pleased how it ended up with Angela coming to visit him. He's not too angry with Jacob anymore."

"I told them both they would suit each other well before they met," Elsa-May said. "I think that they'll get married."

"I think they will too," Emma said. "Robert as *gut* as said so to Angela. They're courting now. I don't think she'd mind me telling you that."

"Is she staying with you for a while longer, Emma?" Maureen asked.

"*Jah*, she's staying on with me. She can't very well go back to Bloomfield now that she's in love with Robert."

"And I've got my *schweschder,* Sabrina, still living with me. I hope she finds a *mann* soon or goes back home," Silvie said. "I'm glad that she turned her attentions away from your Wil, Emma."

"Is she giving you trouble?" Ettie asked Silvie.

Silvie gave an embarrassed laugh. "*Nee*, it's just that I'd grown used to my own company."

Emma knew what Silvie meant. She knew that she could live by herself if she absolutely had to, but was glad that she didn't have to. With Wil as her husband she would be able to have *kinner* and create a proper *familye*. She hoped that being in her late twenties she would not have trouble conceiving a child when the time came. She was glad that Wil had waited for her until enough time had passed to marry another man. Emma was confident that no one would whisper or point fingers at Wil and her for marrying in a few months time. By that time, it would be well over a year since Levi went to be with the Lord. "If

Wil and I marry soon, will I still be welcome at these meetings?"

"*Jah,* of course," Elsa-May said.

"You were once widowed so that's enough to qualify," Ettie said with a grin on her face.

Emma smiled; she was happy that *Gott* had blessed her with *gut* friends and a *wunderbaar mann* with whom she would spend many fun-filled days. She would wait until Angela moved out and then she could concentrate on getting ready to marry Wil at last.

Thank you for reading 'Accused.'

All the books in this series:

ABOUT THE AUTHOR

Samantha Price is a best selling author who knew she wanted to become a writer at the age of seven, while her grandmother read to her Peter Rabbit in the sun room. It is her love of Amish culture that inspires her to write clean and wholesome books, with more than a dash of sweetness. Though she has penned over one hundred and twenty Amish Romance and Amish Mystery books, Samantha is just as in love today with exploring the spiritual and emotional journeys of her characters as she was the day she first put pen to paper. Samantha lives in a quaint Victorian cottage with three rambunctious dogs.

www.samanthapriceauthor.com
samanthaprice333@gmail.com
www.facebook.com/SamanthaPriceAuthor
Follow Samantha Price on BookBub
Twitter @ AmishRomance